BLOOD TITHE

A GOTHIKA NOVEL

TONY FUENTES & C.S. KADING

SANDDANCER PUBLICATIONS

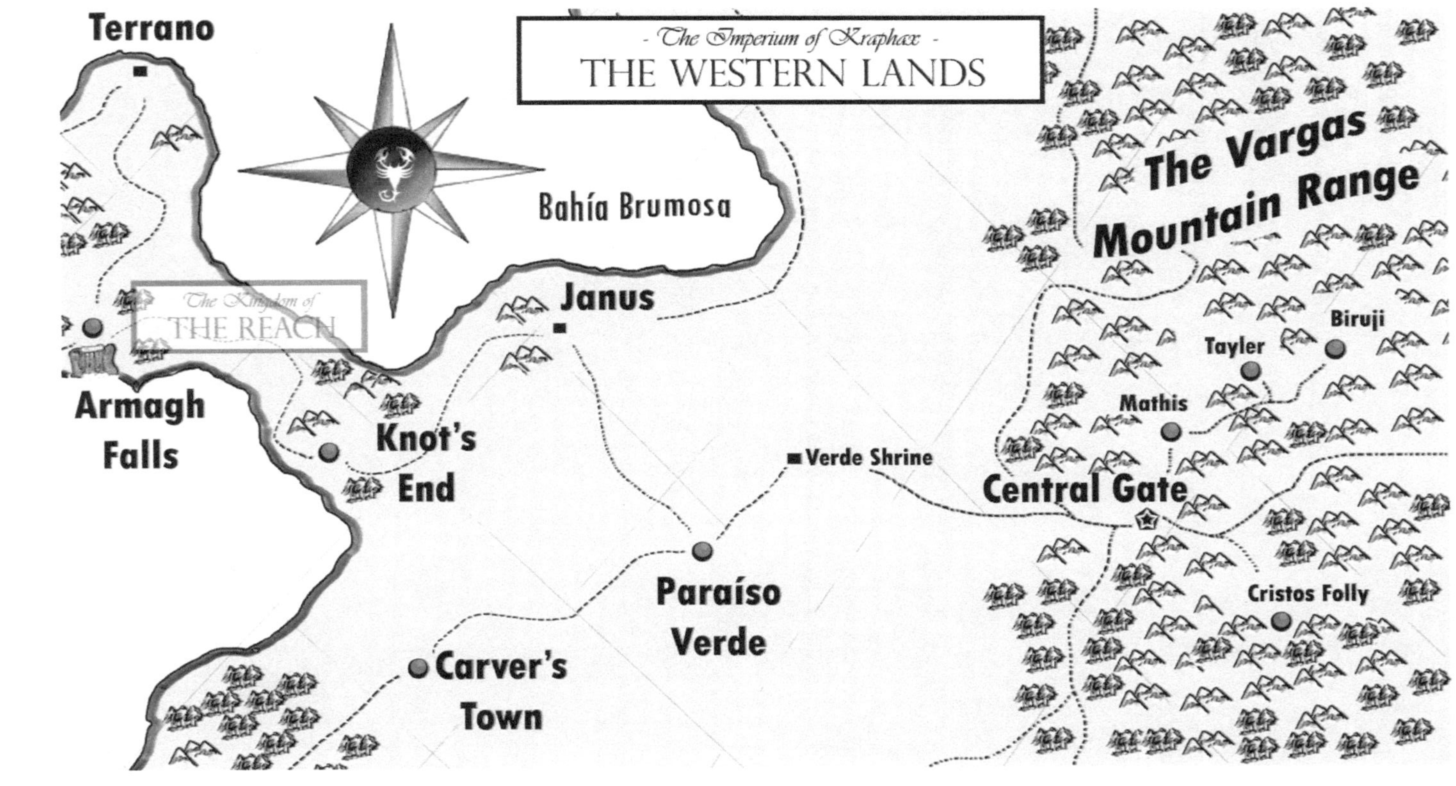

- The Imperium of Kraphax -
THE WESTERN LANDS
Terrano
The Vargas
Mountain Range
Bahía Brumosa
The Kingdom of
THE REACH
Janus
Biruji
Tayler
Armagh
Falls
Mathis
Knot's
End
Verde Shrine
Central Gate
Paraíso
Verde
Cristos Folly
Carver's
Town

Paperback ISBN: 979-8-9852825-9-7

Ebook ISBN: ISBN: 979-8-9852825-8-0

Copyright file: 1-12844363261

Edited by Finley Hislop

Cover and Chapter Headers by Etheric Designs

Layout by Atticus

*This is dedicated to our love of monsters,
in all their varied forms.
Without Fear, Courage could not be found... and Darkness has
no meaning without Light.*

CONTENTS

PARAÍSO VERDE

*H*il preserve me, Henri Cruz thought. *I am going to die.*

His heartbeat thundered in his temples, fueling the ringing in his ears. The immense weight of the wooden chest atop him crushed the air out of him, causing each breath to come in short, ragged bursts. Porcelain shrapnel from the tiny figurines of sheep, bulls, and other animals stuck out of his skin, painfully digging in further as he desperately gasped to refill his lungs. The scent of dust and smoke filled his mouth but there was something else, too. The smell was pungent and powerful, like the scent of unwashed skin and sweat mixed with something foul... something rotting. He swallowed to keep himself from gagging. A tickling sensation teased over his forehead and cheek, wet and worrisome. Henri knew he was bleeding but couldn't tell where or how badly.

The ringing in his ears faded, only to be replaced by the sounds of rabid sniffing and the smacking of wet lips and slavering. The weight above him shifted and excited hissing filled the darkness around him. Fear pinned his limbs in place as the pressure from above increased; more of them were climbing onto his cabinet prison. Breathing grew more painful, a sharp stabbing in his chest as the air vanished from his lungs again. Panic prickled along his neck and Henri became desperate to flee, but the fear of what was above him kept him there. Henri could only imagine their faces sniffing the air like animals. They were searching for something. Were they searching for him?

Henri's life flashed before his eyes, a desperate last bid to find a way out of his situation. A few hours prior, Henri had arrived in the town of Paraíso Verde to buy supplies for the family. They had just celebrated his twenty-second birthday that summer. He had put the errand off all week until his mother threatened to beat him with her shoe. Amusing as the thought was he knew better. He did not want to anger the woman who made the meals for the family. That never ended well.

He had left their small farm near the village after the sun peaked overhead. The trek into town had only taken about an hour. There would have been plenty of time to collect what his family needed for the month and still make a special stop. He had recalled Isabella might be working at the mercantile next to the butcher's shop today, so he'd worn his nice vest over his faded linen shirt and styled his dark hair. Maybe he could talk her into an early supper before he had to return. It would be after dark when he set off, but the Valley had been peaceful for years.

He had just loaded up the wagon with the last of the purchases when he saw it. Two horses raced down the main street towing a blazing carriage. He and everyone else on the street had watched the scene in stunned silence. The daydream-like atmosphere was broken when two passengers jumped from the carriage and landed on the pavement. One passenger had on flashy clothing that suggested they had money. The other person was filthy and unkempt. Their face was covered in deep crimson blood. Henri watched as the person looked up and then all around. Their eyes were black, almost lifeless. Henri had never seen that sort of expression before. The injured person glanced down at their companion and flipped them onto their back. At first, Henri had thought they were smiling but the smile was wrong. It was too wide and too unnerving. Then they bit into their companion's throat. The man convulsed and tried to scream but the only sound was a gurgle as his body shook.

Across the street a woman screamed, drawing Henri's attention away from the scene before him. An unkempt man and woman were running toward the shrieking woman. Like the blood-covered man in the carriage, they wore tattered and dirty clothes. In one swift movement, they knocked their prey to the ground. One bit into her throat and the other bit into the side of her face, tearing the flesh of her cheek away. Henri had forced himself to look away from the increasing carnage. He peered down the street and observed several more of these creatures. They were running impossibly fast and tackling anyone who stood in their path. Somehow, Henri had noticed a single person standing tall on a rooftop while the crowd of creatures approached. He felt the person's eyes upon him, though he could not make out their face.

Terror overwhelmed Henri and he ran back into the butcher's shop, slamming the door behind him. He spun on his heel and saw Koran the Butcher, who had a knife in his hand and a look of fright in his eyes. The paralyzing blend of shrieks and unearthly cries from the outdoors was enough to rattle even the bravest of men.

"I'm bolting the door!" Henri said as he slid the wooden bar into place. "Secure the bar..."

An explosion shook the building, interrupting his sentence. The glass-paneled cabinet had taken him by surprise, blown free from its resting place by the explosion and trapping him beneath it.

"Mr. Cruz? Henri, are you okay?"

Henri could hear the scuffle and crunch of feet against the floor and glass, but it ended the moment he heard Koran's voice cry, "Stay away! All of you stay back!" Henri envisioned Koran holding a huge knife or maybe even two. If Koran could make it to the back, he could take refuge in his cold room. Henri realized the horde had discovered the butcher as Koran's menacing yells became cries of anguish and terror. The butcher's voice faded away and was replaced by the sounds of excited hissing and sniffing, bringing Henri back to his present situation.

The pressure of the cabinet against his chest changed, growing lighter than it had been. The shelves lilted from side to side as a single person deliberately paced the length of his prison. The hissing and sniffing stopped suddenly. Whoever this was, was important. Henri held his breath and tried to remain silent while staring into the darkness. The entity above him paced back and forth, taking its time as if waiting him out. He felt a sudden sting in his eyes and he shut both of them. He thought it was sweat and tried to rub it away, but his fingers caught a piece of shrapnel and spread fresh blood along with the old across his face. A wave of frenzied sniffing and hissing filled the room again.

Blood. They smelled the blood. *His* blood.

They all piled onto the cabinet again and Henri's terror grew. It was only a matter of time before they found him and ate him like they had the others. Only a matter of time before he became one of them. His thoughts were chilling, but he knew he'd rather be dead than there for what was coming.

Evil had resurfaced and all of them were doomed.

The constant jolting of the buckboard made for a very unpleasant journey. Lyric shifted around in the seat beside the Guild driver, trying to find a spot that would not cause her tender backside to bruise any further. The four of them had been on the road together for two days now. The driver at her side had collected her from the University Library in Valle Espino, Thorn Valley, several days before meeting up with the other two in their group.

Lyric carried a simple traveler's pack and bedroll, pocket coin enough for her journey, and the instruments of her calling: pen, ink, and paper. Lyric was an Imperial Scribe. She recorded everything that transpired - no detail too small, no fact too obvious. She recently had her twentieth birthday, signaling that it was time for her Verdad, her "moment of truth." Each servant of the Imperium had to undergo their own Prueba - a search for Truth; this was hers. The outcome of this journey would determine if she succeeded, and could advance to the position of Historian, or if she would remain a simple Scribe for the Library.

The driver seated to her left on the buckboard seat kept her eyes on the road ahead of them, as she had since collecting Lyric from the steps of the Library. Luz Wheeler was a stoic woman and a credit to her Guild. She was pleasant enough and had shared several stories with Lyric along the way. Stories of various encounters that she and her fellow Guild members had experienced along this stretch of road from Valle Espino to Paraíso Verde. Most of these tales involved defending their charges from highwaymen. Lyric wondered if there was some romantic twist on a few of them, based on the twinkle in Luz's eyes as she told them. Occasionally, however, there were encounters far less pleasant. Encounters involving creatures and creations from a war some three hundred years passed.

The Corpse Wars.

It was because of these potential encounters that the other two travelers were part of this detail. Individuals trained to handle the remnants of the War. Remnants that often included the undead.

Lyric moved a bit and put her hip on the side of the seat to ease some of the strain and then looked at her two traveling acquaintances, who were sitting in the back of the wagon.

The Inquisition of Hil was formed during the height of the Corpse Wars. They were persons called to serve the God Hil, the personification of Light and Creation. Regardless of sex or gender, those called into Hil's Faithful Service swore to defend the living from the taint of evil and undeath. Scribes were tenderly invited to join a mission alongside Hil's most faithful. It gave them an appreciation for the world that existed beyond the protection of high walls and palace guards.

The woman introduced herself as Esperanza Boyorquez, a healer, and Voice for Hil's most faithful. She had a peaceful demeanor that was both calming and reassuring. Her dark hair was pulled back into a tight, no-nonsense bun. Her vestments were simple and unadorned; an off-white linen robe over which was an equally unassuming thigh-length tunic dyed a faded saffron yellow-orange. The over-tunic was split up the side to allow movement, and the full-length sleeves were rolled up to her elbows, displaying a soft tan cotton lining.

Where Esperanza brought a sense of comfort, the person she was with, Jalin Cortez, did not. He sat with a pocket stone in hand and was honing a long blade. His leather pants were stained with road dirt, oil, and other things Lyric dared not ask about. Various stitches and patch jobs covered his pants, showing either a lack of wealth or a predisposition to getting the most out of an object before discarding it. His threadbare cotton shirt was worn open at the neck, hints of scarred flesh peering out from within. Across his lap was draped a leather long coat, equally worn and patched. A pair of goggles with multiple lenses hung around his neck. An unruly mop of hair was slicked back and held in place at the nape of his neck with a tight leather thong. If Lyric considered him long enough, she would have to describe his features, like his clothing: well worn.

Lyric had observed the two of them for the past several hours as they sat across from each other in an almost palpable silence. The woman had a sober expression. Lyric noticed her subtle body language; feet turned slightly away, eyes half-lidded, chin tilted ever-so-slightly up. Esperanza Boyorquez wanted nothing to do with Jalin Cortez.

Two days back, when they had collected the pair of Inquisitors and the supplies in the back of the wagon, the sky had been a blend of dark lilac and sky blue. It was supposed to be a basic supply run to some outlying Shrines. Nothing adventurous. Nothing calling for a full retinue or compliment of attendants. A simple task along an established trade route. The perfect mission for a young Scribe to experience the outside world, before being cloistered away again with her books and manuscripts.

The sun had yet to peek over the horizon as the wagon clattered and bounced across a long wooden bridge. Lyric tucked a red curl back behind her ear that had come dislodged in the jostling of the ride. The water below the bridge added to the chill of the sunless sky overhead. She wished she had thought to pack a hat.

Boyorquez tucked her hands under her arms for warmth. Her eyes examined the man across from her for a moment and then fixated on a place on the horizon. Lyric had the feeling Boyorquez wanted nothing more than to push Cortez off the wagon and into the river. She marveled at the peculiar coupling and wondered what had happened between them to cause Boyorquez to clearly detest her partner.

Lyric's green eyes wandered over to the figure of Cortez. Currently, he wasn't engaging in anything particularly objectionable. He was simply sharpening his blade. A blade whose edge could have easily split a hair, yet Cortez continued to sharpen its deadly edge. It seemed simple weapons upkeep.

Esperanza Boyorquez's official title was the Voice of Hil, but the title meant more than just a specific form of address. The Faithful of Hil came in many forms. A few were extraordinarily devout, while some had difficulty with basic prayer and worship. By Hil's blessing, Esperanza was granted the power to use Their Gifts to defeat those who defiled the world of the living. She carried Hil's Voice within her mortal frame.

Jalin Cortez was a different story.

The Ministry of Hil had long ago realized the need for strong hands and cold hearts. Cortez was not touched by Hil. He was not blessed with any divine or magical gifts. What he was, was extremely proficient in mercenary work and deeply devout.

Lyric had asked Luz one evening about their escorts. In a guarded tone, the driver had shared that Cortez was rumored to have weathered a lycanthrope pandemic, battled a ghoul infestation, and extinguished three rogue mages, one being a Fire Singer. Whispers followed his name, "killer" and "murderer." But to the Chosen of Hil, he was simply Justice.

With the intention of either complicating the situation or easing the atmosphere, Lyric was not entirely sure of which, Jalin began to softly whistle as he worked. The tune was difficult to decipher. It could have been filled with sorrow, regret, or even acceptance. Looking up, he made eye contact with Esperanza and smiled at her. It was not an earnest smile. It was the smile of someone who knew he was hated and did not care.

Lyric watched as he continued to sharpen his scoring blade. That wasn't the correct name for the weapon. It was a form of short sword. A thin blade with a razor-sharp edge. Cortez's scoring blade was unique. Strapped to his forearm, it was locked in a specialized set of gears. With the correct movement, the sharpened metal would snap forward, and the extended blade would lock in place. This extension would allow its user to move the blade with a more refined accuracy in a fight. Its blade bore not only steel but a silvered treatment, as well as the blessing of the Hil. Such gifts made it a formidable weapon in his hands.

Lyric cast a glance over her shoulder, smiling as if she hadn't noticed the disagreement between the Inquisitors. "I apologize, Inquisitor Cortez, but what is the tune? It sounds beautiful; does it have any words?"

Cortez looked up and for a moment and weighed the Scribe's words, as if trying to gauge her sincerity. Staring at her, he managed to politely force out, "It is… it is an older song."

Lyric could tell Cortez was used to having his methods questioned, but asking about his off-duty habits confused him. While not detrimental, it was a small piece of information that she made certain to take note of.

"It's beautiful, sir," Lyric said in thanks and turned her attention back to the road. She remembered her grandparent's quiet arguments. There was no yelling, just busy work, and distraction. She remembered watching her grandmother angrily folding hand towels toward her grandfather. Nary a word was exchanged, but the sentiment was conveyed.

"Signs up ahead say that we should hit Paraíso Verde shortly. Smoke ahead says within the…" Luz paused, and took a deep inhale, scenting the wind and the smoke. The Guild driver turned and looked at Lyric and then back to the pair of Inquisitors, "There may be an issue."

Cortez and Boyorquez looked up at each other, their unspoken battles fallen to the wayside at that moment, then back at the driver. "Proceed with haste," Esperanza ordered.

Whipping the horses, the wagon lurched forward with increased speed. Lyric felt the tension that had plagued them the last two days fade. She sensed fear emanating from Luz. Cortez's excitement was increasing - his instinct for the hunt was being triggered by signs of trouble. He was already taking out a pack and strapping on his gear. Esperanza's face was filled with fear and worry.

As their wagon sped along toward its destination, Lyric tried to recall what she knew about the village ahead.

Paraíso Verde was not a simple hamlet. It was an agricultural and farming center for the area. Cattle and grain were both provided from the rich and fertile valley. While not as wealthy as the Kingdom of the Reach, Paraíso Verde's soil was the richest on this side of the Vargas Mountain Range. It was also the final agricultural settlement along the southern border of the Imperium, before the rocky peninsula of The Reach. The only thing south of this location was the small township of Carver's Town and the border Outpost Ultimo. Carver's Town was a village that consisted of a handful of families. They all worked and lived together in their communal town center. Unlike Paraíso Verde, where many families controlled vast acreages of land and came into town to do their business. The Outpost was a military installation overseen by the Imperium and the Kingdom of the Reach. A minor trade outpost, it acted as a point of first engagement if there were any issues with the Kaxians to the far south.

Lyric considered the smoke ahead of them and their location. Should this be the Kaxians, then this supply run could be the first warning of an act of war.

WITCHCRAFT

Torched buildings, broken glass, and blood splatter greeted them upon their arrival. After a quick pass down the main road through the village, Luz found a defensible place to park the wagon and horses. The group exited the wagon, eyes scanning the area as they did so.

Cortez removed a long gun from the wagon's storage area. He skimmed it quickly, loaded it, and then glanced over at Lyric and Luz.

"While not of the Faith, I am confident that representatives of the Imperium and the Guild will take my advice seriously. Work together, bring a weapon, and don't be fooled by what you see. A victim's face can be worn by an abomination, figuratively and literally. Do you understand these instructions?"

Despite the anxious atmosphere, Cortez's voice was full of determination and confidence.

"Ms. Wax, you have less hunting experience, I assume." Cortez looked over at Lyric. She replied with a simple head nod. "Then you are with me."

Lyric considered his words and the situation. No area was completely safe since the end of the Corpse Wars. Even after nearly three centuries, remnants of the armies of the dead still roamed the lands. Incursions into more civilized regions of the Imperium had decreased in number over the years, as Hil's Faithful located the monsters and put them to rest. But the only truly safe place to be was behind the tall walls of the Imperial Palace. Even then, rumors of unsavory happenings still occurred, though they were often quickly dismissed as nothing more than that... rumors.

Lyric's University peers had focused on forecasting when and where these remnant pockets would appear, based on the historical data and accounts from Hunters, Inquisitors, Peace Keepers, and eyewitnesses. That information was then handed off to persons like Cortez and Boyorquez who would be dispatched with a retinue to handle the problem and restore peace to the area. Paraíso Verde had not been on those charts when Lyric accepted this assignment.

She was not prepared for this.

Cortez handed out a pair of pistols to Lyric and Luz with extra rounds of ammunition.

Luz gave an exasperated snort regarding Cortez's actions and returned the pistol. She reached up to her seat on the carriage and pulled down her own firearm and blade.

"Guild doesn't let us drive if we don't know how to defend... Inquisitor." She replied.

Ignoring the comment, Jalin glanced at Esperanza. She appeared to be waiting, or in contemplation. He sucked on his tooth and then nodded.

She wrapped her long fingers around the sun-shaped pendant hanging from her neck and held the Sigil of Hil in her hand. The symbol, a blazing red sun, glowed slightly as she asked for Their Favor.

"Hil's Light, grant me your vision," she whispered. A wave of warmth spread outward from Esperanza. Her eyes glowed a radiant gold. She gazed up and down the street, her golden eyes examining everything around them.

A wrinkle formed between her eyebrows, followed by a narrowing of her eyes.

"What is it? Is there something there?" Luz asked. Her honey-colored eyes darted from doorway to doorway.

Esperanza shook her head. "No. The dead... there is... nothing," she said with a bit of astonishment. "By all rights, the amount of blood on the ground, and destruction in the area, should have produced a shade or spirit... someone still clinging to this world... who could have relayed the tale or two of what happened. Yet..."

"Then we do it without witchcraft." He hefted his rifle upwards and peered through the scoping mechanism that was affixed to the top and surveyed the street.

Lyric watched the actions of both inquisitors, noting Cortez's choice of phrase to refer to Esperanza's gifts.

Witchcraft.

The Divine bestowed their Gifts sparingly upon mortals. It was not something that could be learned through studying, no matter how much time was invested. Such Gifts were treated as a blessing by most people. Although these abilities had a Divine origin, some saw them as an abomination that should not be tolerated.

The Death Mages and the Corpse Wars had only cemented those superstitions.

Lyric looked between the two Inquisitors for a moment. *Perhaps this was the source of their discontent.*

She examined the pistol that Cortez had placed in her hands, meticulously loading it with care, and attempted to shake off the thought. Dissecting their relationship was not important right now. She needed to focus. She needed to follow his lead.

Cortez motioned for Lyric to accompany him, and for Esperanza and Luz to survey the opposite end of the street. He gestured to her to keep her eyes on the buildings on the right while he watched the left. He narrowed his eyes and scanned the buildings for movement. There was none. The acrid smell of smoke filled the air. The fading light cast an eerie glow on the landscape.

Something, or possibly several somethings, had caused this carnage.

Cortez pulled on a pair of goggles then reached up to his left eye and flipped a lens down. His vision shifted slightly. The fire cast a warm, orange glow across the area. The lens would allow him to see the heat from bodies. He could detect the slightest movement, even if it was cold and still. He could see the heat radiating from his hand on the firearm and glimpsed Lyric in his peripheral. Esperanza and her ilk were gifted with Hil's illuminating light, which allowed them to see what otherwise might not be seen. He was not endowed with any special talents, so he had to rely on the quality of craftsmanship and training to even the odds.

His face contorted into a scowl, his eyebrows furrowing with irritation.

"What do you see, Ms. Wax?" he asked.

Lyric jumped a little at his comment.

"I see fire, broken glass..." she paused. "I see blood, but no bodies."

Jalin nodded. Blood splattered doorways and windows, and slick red trails on cobblestone led into alleyways and buildings. She was right, there were no bodies.

"Animals?" he asked. His long legs carried him down the street smoothly. He gestured to a building and carefully stepped toward it.

Lyric shook her head and said nothing.

Jalin nodded and pressed his narrow shoulders against the side of the building by the open door. Force had been used to open it. It lay shattered in the entryway in a flurry of splinters. He gestured for Lyric to remain where she was, against the wall, away from the door. He inhaled deeply.

Smoke. Wood smoke. Pine. He thought. He caught a faint whiff of something metallic, like an old copper penny, on the back of his nose.

Copper. Blood. A lot of it. But the sweet scent of roasting flesh or the sharp tint of singed hair did not accompany it. If there was a body here, it was not on fire. A small gust of wind caused the hairs on his neck to stand on end. He needed to get in closer.

Quietly shouldering his long gun, he flicked his left arm out. His scoring blade snapped into place, its silvery surface weakly reflecting the light from above as the smoke made the bright morning gray. He raised it to his eyes and angled the mirrored blade to reflect the room within.

Broken furniture, shattered glassware, and scattered foodstuffs littered the mercantile. A cast-iron frying pan lay in the middle of the blood splatter. He glanced inside quickly and scanned the area. Nothing and no one. The room remained empty.

Cortez nodded to Lyric and stepped inside, quickly approaching the area where signs of a fight had taken place. He squatted and examined the evidence, careful not to touch anything.

Lyric whispered to Jalin from the doorway, "Shouldn't we keep looking?"

Jalin ignored the scribe's inquiry. Someone had tried to fight back here. A chunk of matted hair decorated the edge of the frying pan. Whoever it was had connected with their assailant, and this might be what he needed to know what they were up against.

He glanced up from his location, scanning the room once more. Searching for anything that might hide in the corners or the rafters. Satisfied with his assessment, he carefully unlocked his blade and moved it back into the ready position. Setting his long gun aside, he quickly donned a pair of leather gloves sealed in beeswax. He reached for the matt of hair on the edge of the pan. The waxy coating would briefly prevent the blood from seeping through the leather and protect him from exposure. It was long enough for him to deposit the sample into one of the many empty glass vials he had tucked into his belt.

Cortez pulled the hair loose from the iron with skilled fingers and quickly uncorked a vial with his clean glove, then scooped the sample into its clear cage and sealed it shut. Pulling the soiled glove off and peeling it away from his skin, he examined his bare hand carefully under the gaze of his monocle. He set the glove aside and removed the other using its uncontaminated surface to collect the soiled garment and seal it away in an oiled leather bag, which was then stored in another oiled leather bag.

Jalin noted Lyric's presence as she approached. He did not need to look up at her to know that she was curious.

"Samples," he said. "Once we know we are in a safe place, I can analyze them and hopefully confirm what we are dealing with."

"Do you think it might be ghouls?" Lyric asked.

Jalin shook his head and recovered his long gun. "Ghouls are messy, and leave corpses. They also stink. No scent of rotten meat in the area and…" he gestured to the blood splatter. "No corpse." He considered for a moment. "It is possible they could be controlled and are collecting their victims."

Lyric's breath hissed as she inhaled sharply. "A Death Mage? I thought…"

"They were all gone?" Jalin cut her off. "We have a University dedicated to their education, thanks to the Imperator's son." he scowled and spat. "Never assume we have them all corralled. It only ever takes one to break ranks, and we have the Corpse Wars all over again."

Lyric's face paled at the thought.

The Imperium had been free of the terror of the Death Mages for almost 300 years. By the Imperator's grace, and with the help of Hil's most fervent believers, those who dared to bring the forces of the dead against the Imperium of Kraphax had been destroyed. Most of the armies of the dead had fallen into disarray or collapsed entirely with the deaths of those who controlled them. Most was not all. Clusters of undead still roamed the land, infecting the living with their impurity. They had to be found and exterminated, lest a new plague of the damned walked free once more.

To prevent such an occurrence from happening again, the Imperium had ordered the elimination of all those associated with the Ars Necromantia. Despite their successful purge, the ability to see and speak with the dead persisted. Styx continued to give Their Gifts to humanity.

Imperator Isodoro's son Travaren had been one such child so born. Isodoro, who became the third Imperator of Kraphax, had no magical background. Neither had his wife. Isodoro commanded that Traveran's bloodline be investigated, to affirm Travaren was his son. It proved true. There had been no explanation, other than it was the work of the Gods.

It had been a bitter pill for all to swallow. The gifts of Styx, much like those of Hil, could not be disregarded or refused.

Or controlled.

Travaren's Gifts of Styx assured he could never assume the throne. After the Corpse Wars, trust in Death Mages was negligible. No one would stand for him as Imperator. In a gesture of humility and respect for his Imperial father, he stepped away from the throne and renounced his claim to it. To ensure those born with the Gifts of Styx were properly informed on how to use them, Travaren established a University where they could receive formal education. Raised under Hil's watchful eye, and in Hil's Light, these Necromists, as they were renamed, would serve Hil and the Imperium in ways their darker predecessors never had.

It was rumored there were now fewer than a dozen of these magicians in existence. They were as rare as they were dangerous. The thought that one of them might be responsible for the senseless slaughter of this town was unsettling.

It was also terrifying.

Cortez and Boyorquez were trained in the duties of protection and perseverance. Called to the service of Hil, they wielded faith and fire to help cleanse the realm of impurities such as these. But as much as it was an honor, it was also a curse. Inquisitors of Hil rarely died of old age or infirmity. Theirs was a calling of battle, and most often died at the claws and fangs of the very creatures they sought to protect humankind from.

The sound of a booted footfall on the wooden planks outside caught Cortez's ear. In a single swift movement, he stood, stepped to Lyric's side, and aimed his weapon, placing himself between the Scribe and the door.

"Cortez?" Boyorquez's voice called softly from the other side of the open doorway.

Cortez's thumb pulled the hammer back on his long gun. It clicked loudly.

"Hil's light sees all," Boyorquez said.

Cortez's shoulders relaxed slightly. "No stone unturned." He replied and lowered the muzzle of his weapon to the ground.

"Clear," he said.

Boyorquez, followed by Luz, stepped into the mercantile. The female Inquisitor's eyes scanned the area, falling on the same scene that had drawn the attention of her partner.

"No survivors?" she asked.

Cortez shook his head. "None. Shades?" he asked her.

She shook her head. "Not a one."

He grimaced at the comment, fished the oiled leather bag out, and tossed it onto a table next to Boyorquez. "Caught some hair and a blood sample off of a frying pan. Someone put up a fight before going down."

"Cast iron?"

He nodded.

"So not the... the Children," she said. There was a moment of hesitation in her voice. Superstition said that creatures had power in their names, and to call upon those names would easily invite misfortune.

Cortez made a face. "Monsters. They are just monsters, and if they were involved in this, we are under-prepared." He said.

"Is anyone ever truly prepared for them?" she asked softly.

Cortez gave a non-committal lift of his shoulders. He nodded at the bag with his chin and pursed his lips, pointing at it.

"Think you can pull someone back to ask questions?"

Boyorquez's eyes fell on the small bundle.

"Maybe."

"Then do what needs doing." He said and moved to the door.

"Not staying to help?" she asked, stepping up to the table.

"Unless Hil's word has decreed that my presence is required while you practice your witchcraft, I will remain outside," came the reply.

"The blessings of Hil are not witchcraft, Cortez."

"And the blessings of Styx are not necromancy," he countered, "Or so the Imperator's son would have us believe. You bruja are all the same." He stepped over the shattered remains of the door and out into the street.

SILENCE OF THE DEAD

Esperanza's eyes never left Cortez as he departed. Her expression was stoic, and no words escaped her lips. Inhaling a calming breath, she paused for a moment and then exhaled slowly.

Lyric looked on after Cortez and then glanced back at Esperanza.

"Can I be of assistance?" the young woman asked. Beside her, Luz scoffed and leaned against the doorframe.

"He's an asshole," Luz said of Cortez. "How did you get saddled with him?" she asked Esperanza.

"A Hand needs a Voice and a Voice needs a Hand." The woman shrugged slightly. "It is the way of things."

Luz pursed her lips at the non-committal comment. "Watch your back with that one, hermana. I hear that the blood on his hands isn't always from the undead."

"Unproven speculation," Esperanza replied. She moved around the room to inspect it, then added softly, "But your concern is appreciated."

"Wait," Lyric began, "Are you implying that Inquisitor Cortez…"

"Is rumored to be responsible for the injuries of the other Vocas he has been assigned to?" Luz interjected. She pushed herself off the wall and shook her head. "No. Not implying at all."

"A conversation for another time." Esperanza cut in. "Regardless of his personal leanings, Cortez was right about one thing… if there was a witness, I might be able to use those remains to bring them back."

Luz made a warding gesture against evil and swore softly under her breath.

"I thought…" Lyric said, "I thought only Necromists could speak with the dead?"

Esperanza shrugged once more and cleaned off the top of a table.

"Styx, who governs the underworld, grants gifts related to the afterlife and death. Death and dying are present in healing and medicine… tools used to stop death and dying." She looked at Lyric. "Did you know that many of those blessed by Styx are physicians, skilled in the medical arts?"

Confused, Lyric shook her head, "No. I was unaware."

Esperanza continued. She walked around the perimeter of the table as she spoke.

"Hil's gifts illuminate, bring life, and provide clarity to replace both darkness and confusion. Their Gifts allow people to search for what was hidden and to bring it openly into the world."

She passed around the edges of the table a second time.

"Sometimes those hidden things are shades and ghosts, trapped in this realm and unable to travel to the Place Beyond. A select few of Hil's chosen... myself included...can access the Lord of Light's strength and locate those lost souls."

She walked around it a third time.

"It is here that the Gifts of Hil and the Gifts of Styx sometimes converge, each controlling aspects of the dead." She paused a moment and looked toward the doorway, where Cortez had exited. "Many are offended by such things, despite their Divine origins."

A dawning realization came to Lyric. This is what the two Inquisitors were arguing about! Esperanza was Gifted with talents Cortez considered profane. He was trying to catch her in a misstep and she was trying to do her job!

Esperanza ceased her walk around the table as she completed its third circuit. She placed the remains that Cortez had given her in the center of the table. She reached into the bag at her hip. Carefully selecting a piece of chalk, she inscribed the wooden table with a few symbols. Symbols of protection. Symbols of power. Then, out of another pouch, she drizzled a thin line of salt to encircle her drawings.

The Imperial Scribe's eyes widened in awe as they tracked Esperanza's graceful movements. Lyric watched as the Inquisitor held Hil's symbol and whispered over the table. The words were spoken with a hushed reverence, like a whisper in the night. Her body glowed with a golden-reddish hue, and soon the symbols began to shimmer and sparkle.

In the tongue of her faith, Esperanza called to the soul to show itself to the living.

Lyric caught herself holding her breath in anticipation.

There was nothing.

Esperanza frowned. Her brown knit as she focused once more. The air warmed. The table rumbled as the power was directed into the symbols.

Once again, nothing came forth.

The Voca exhaled a frustrated breath.

"Something is not right," she said. She released her grip on her medallion and stepped toward the table.

Taking a look at the small package in the center, she reached out and lifted it up. Unlatching it, she let the contents slide out into the center of the circle. She stared at it a moment. Then looked over at Luz.

The Driver blanched and held up their hands in defense. "No."

"I need to see something, come here." Esperanza gestured.

Luz clenched her jaw and took a couple of hesitant steps forward.

Esperanza reached into her belt and drew out a small knife. Luz flinched.

"It's not for you." The Inquisitor commented. She continued to stare at Luz's hairline and then glanced back at the flap of skin and hair on the table. "Hrmm" she mused.

"What do you see, Inquisitor?" Lyric asked, her green eyes sparkled with curiosity.

"It would have been difficult to tear the skin from a body using a cast iron skillet." Esperanza reached out with her knife and flipped the skin to reveal the flesh underneath. She was careful not to touch it with her hands. She shook her head.

"That's not right." she said and then called out to Cortez, "Inquisitor Cortez, a moment if you will."

Cortez made his way back inside. His typically disdainful expression shifted suddenly to one of confusion. "No ghost?"

"No. Even with two summonings."

"Then what do you want from me?" he demanded.

Esperanza glowered at the man. " Take another look at the sample. I think we may have an issue."

Lyric shifted her position from where she stood, to give both Inquisitors the room they needed. She wanted to see what they were doing and witness what they were discussing. But she also realized that this was not a sterile laboratory and this was not a controlled specimen. They were in the field, and this was a hostile location. She chewed on the inside of her cheek and peered in their direction.

Cortez frowned at Esperanza's request but then reached into his jacket and pulled out a soft black leather pouch. He opened it and extracted a simple pair of reading glasses and a handkerchief. Gently placing the glasses on the bridge of his nose, he draped the cloth over his mouth and carefully leaned in.

He frowned and paused and leaned back. Glancing away his eyes fell on an oil lamp on a shelf.

"Ms. Wax, would you be so kind as to bring me some light?" he asked.

"Of course!" Lyric said. She knew that Esperanza could have provided light for them, through her magical Gifts. She also knew that Cortez would never ask for them.

She recovered the lamp from its place on the shelf, lit it with her pocket firesteele, and returned to his side.

Cortez nodded in thanks and glanced at Esperanza. "Without witchcraft."

She dismissed his comment and gestured back to the table. "Well?"

"Hrmmm" he mused, once more turning his attention to the sample. He gestured for Lyric to move closer. She obliged. He paused a moment and then retrieved what looked like a long, thin pin or nail from the pouch. He carefully probed the under the flesh. Only a few droplets of blood lingered within the thin layers of muscles.

"There isn't any," he said.

"There isn't any what?" Lyric asked.

"Fatty tissue," he answered. "If I were to skin a creature, certain tissue bits remain attached underneath. Even with a blow from the cast iron, we should have seen a small chunk of the skull still attached. There wasn't anything. So the flesh had already taken on necrosis," he said grimly.

"Meaning that it was dead already?" Lyric asked.

"Meaning that it may be... as you surmised earlier... ghouls." His eyes locked on Esperanza, "Which means it also may be a Necromancer."

Just then, they heard a whisper of a moan from behind them. Guns were drawn and, with a quick spark, a bright golden-red flame sprung from Boyorquez's hand. The whole room was filled with light.

"IN THE NAME OF HIL, SHOW YOURSELF!" she called.

Near an opening in the wall, that connected the mercantile to the butcher next door, a fallen cabinet shifted. Cortez eased himself alongside the fallen piece of furniture. He looked back at the others, raised three fingers, placed his boot on the edge of the cabinet, braced himself, and slowly counted down from three.

On one, he launched the cabinet upwards to reveal its hidden occupants.

Inside the cabinet was a man, his face covered in dried blood, his body misshapen and broken.

Cortez flicked his arm out and drew his blade once again. He held it close to the mouth of the man and narrowed his eyes. The silvered surface fogged ever so slightly.

"Hold!" Cortez called out, as the man was breathing. "He's alive."

Extinguishing the flame in her hand, Boyorquez darted to his side and quietly chanted over him. Her eyes took on a light golden hue once more, then she stopped. She looked up at the other Inquisitor and shook her head.

"He's dying. His chest is crushed, and his back is broken. He's too far gone for my skills. I can ease his pain, but I cannot save him."

"Is it too late to ask him what happened?" Jalin asked.

Esperanza glared at Jalin. She turned back to the broken man and knelt beside him. She reached out to him and cautiously took his hand into her own.

"Can you hear me? You're safe now," she soothed.

A pained moan escaped his lips, and slowly his eyes opened, "Is .. Isa ..bella.."

"No, I'm sorry. My name is Esperanza. I'm..." she started but was cut off as the man convulsed. His grip on her hand tightened.

With pained words and blood seeping from his mouth, "... they... blood." Another violent shake as he stared into Esperanza's eyes. They were full of terror. Then nothing. The light and the shaking both ceased at once. He was gone.

A few moments of silence ensued before Cortez finally spoke. "Is he still around?"

Esperanza grit her teeth at the comment and glared at Cortez.

He shrugged and motioned back to the body. "Unless you have a better idea?"

Taking a measured breath, she closed her eyes. Intoning the words once again, she searched the room for the soul of the dead man. There was nothing. His spirit had moved on from this world. Looking back at her counterpart, she shook her head.

Cortez kicked at the remains of a countertop in frustration. "The ONE TIME we NEED a damn ghost and nothing wants to poke its head up." He pointed at the Scribe. "Wax, you're coming with me. Maybe we can see if we have any other cabinet dwellers. Someone or something in this town has to know something!"

Looking back at Luz and Boyorquez, Lyric nodded and followed Cortez back out into the street.

"What do we do now?" Luz asked.

Esperanza stared at the dead man and said one final prayer before turning back to Luz, "We keep looking and then we head to the only place we can... the Verde Shrine. And we hope that whatever happened here has not happened there."

There were no other survivors to be found. Blood, broken glass, and signs of struggle were their only reward.

With every empty building, Cortez's mood became darker and more irritated. They were surrounded by evidence of death and destruction but could find no clues as to its source. No bodies. No bones. No viscera.

The best clues they discovered were also the most troublesome. They found several sets of footprints in the mud behind one outbuilding.

He knelt and examined the prints in the drying mud. Blood had mixed with the earth here, giving the ground an almost terracotta color. He pursed his lips and sucked on his teeth.

"One set of boots. Three barefoot. Could be teens... or possibly women." he stood. His eyes followed the tracks, gauging the length of the strides. The tracks were marred in several places.

"They were dragging something."

"Or someone?" Lyric offered quietly.

Cortez looked over at the young Scribe and considered her a moment. Then nodded. "More than likely." He looked back down at the tracks, his eyes following them back to their place of origin. An outhouse. The door dangled off of its hinges, held precariously in place with a single nail. They'd broken the door and dragged whoever was inside out.

"Whatever they are, they are determined… and thorough," he said.

"Reflective of intelligence." She offered.

"Precisely." He gazed skyward for a moment. "We need to get back to the wagon. We found all that we could here," he said and gestured down the road where the wagon was still parked. He could see the other two women walking up from the opposite direction.

"Can we make it to the Shrine before evening?" Lyric asked as she fell in step at Cortez's side.

He nodded. "Barring anything unforeseen, it's less than 3 hours from here."

"And if we don't?" Lyric asked.

"Then we get our answers either way."

Down the road, Luz walked quietly at Esperanza's side. Guild drivers were trained to defend their charges from a variety of mishaps along the road. But this situation was something that the Inquisitor would not have wished on anyone. She and Cortez were trained to battle dispatch the foul, the corrupt, and even the unholy, but the implications of this discovery stretched even her training.

They had spent hours combing through the remains of the buildings, but there was nothing to be found. Streaks of blood and drag marks told a story that words need not convey. If there had been survivors, they were dragged away.

No one escaped.

"Do you believe it was a Necromancer, Inquisitor?" Luz asked quietly.

Esperanza mulled over her answer to the question. When she glanced up, she saw Jalin and the Scribe advancing towards the wagon from the opposite direction. They were still well outside of earshot. She shook her head.

"Despite Inquisitor Cortez's conviction in the matter... no. I do not believe it is. All of this was too clean."

Luz's left eyebrow quirked upward.

"If this carnage was clean, I don't want to know what dirty means," she muttered.

"Ah." Esperanza nodded and explained, "The fact we only found a single skin sample and no other human remains means there was a controlling intelligence in play. Certainly, a Necromancer of old could control hundreds of the undead by their will alone. The gifts of Styx are powerful. However, to possess the ability to order the dead to remove all evidence from their attack?" She shook her head once more. "That would exert too much will, too much power. Not to mention the time needed to verify your minions did the job correctly. The blood here is still too fresh for that level of fastidiousness."

She sighed and continued walking. "Ghouls would attack like pack animals, and maybe they could drag away a few poor souls. But less than a dozen buildings with no survivors? No remains? Ghouls are not clean in their chosen means of feeding. No. Even if a Necromancer could reign them in, there would still be survivors... somewhere. How they missed the single survivor in the cabinet when they found everyone else still puzzles me. It must have been the blood from the butcher's shop that disguised his scent."

Luz nodded as they walked together toward the wagon. The horses were unhitched, in case they needed to escape from some hungry creature. They remained where they were left, ears twitching nostrils flaring but still on duty.

"It was unfortunate that the survivor did not have more to say," Luz commented. They approached the horses and Luz carefully worked to hitch them back up to the wagon.

Esperanza nodded in agreement and pulled herself up onto the driver's seat. "'They' and 'Blood' could mean many things. Neither descriptive enough to make plans off of."

Finishing the last of the yoke traces, Luz hopped back into the driver's seat. Taking the driving lines, she clicked at the horses and they slowly clopped down the road toward Cortez and Lyric.

"I don't like any of this," Cortez said as he walked around the back side of the wagon as it came to a stop. Unlatching the back, he opened it and motioned for Lyric to get on. The Scribe handed him the borrowed pistol before pulling herself up and into the back with the rest of the supplies.

Turning around, Lyric reached out and offered her hand to him. "Sir?"

Jalin hesitated, his gaze shifting momentarily from the hand that was presented to him to the face of the Scribe. A young woman, her skin fair and her hair in curls the same shade as polished copper, smiled back at him. Her eyes were like the meadowgrass that had just been blessed by a spring rain, and they held an untouched innocence.

He placed the pistol back in her hand.

"Keep your eyes open," he said. He pulled himself up and sat with his back to them all, feet hanging over the edge, eyes scanning the horizon.

Rapping the edge of the wagon wall twice with his fist, he simply called out, "To the Shrine."

STONEBRIDGE

H il's faith preferred to construct their Shrines on the highest natural point outside the boundaries of a settlement. A Shrine was a holy place to come and reflect, finding solace and joy in Hil's magnificence. It was not a place where noises and distractions from places of commerce were welcome.

This location choice meant that Shrines to Hil could be seen from many miles away and that they had an unobstructed view in all directions. It made them a focal point on the horizon. Although it gave them a defensible position, it also made them a visible target.

The Verde Shrine sat atop the tallest of a series of rolling hills several leagues outside Paraíso Verde. In the wake of the Corpse Wars, the place was named "Green Paradise" by the settlers that arrived here three hundred years ago. Its soil was rich, and its waters clear. Both of these gifts were a welcome relief for those who had endured the horrific battles of the Death Mages and their undead hordes.

A nearby waterfall dropped into the valley of Paraíso Verde, supplying the Rio Vide with life-giving water for the farmlands and settlements below.

There was no cart path leading up to the Shrine. Horses, carts, wagons, and buggies were all required to be left at the bottom of the hill and pilgrims made the journey up the well-trodden path to the venerated Verde Shrine. Those who could not ascend the hill on their own could take advantage of the lift, which was operated by the energy of the waterfall, in order to reach the courtyard of the Shrine. It also provided a service of delivering supplies from the base of the hill to the pinnacle.

Luz directed the horses off the road and into an area set aside for wheeled transport. There were no other vehicles parked in the staging area. On the horizon, the smoke from the village was still visible, a hazy reminder of the destruction. If someone had attempted to flee the village for the safety of the Shrine, surely their horses and vehicles would be here.

Lyric peered past Luz and Esperanza at the empty staging area for the Shrine. She furrowed her copper-colored eyebrows as the absence of other horses, carts, or people made the atmosphere feel heavy and oppressive. The young woman looked at Esperanza.

"Did no one else make it this far?" She asked.

Esperanza pressed her lips together in a tight line. The idea of that possibility clearly troubled her.

She looked around the area for signs of other travelers. There were none. The Shrine was absent of any animals usually used for transportation. No horse, donkey, or ox was present. An emergency would have surely called the laypeople to action. That could explain the absence of animals from their posts and corrals. But they had seen no one else on the road. There were neither wagons nor carriages. Theirs were the only vehicle here.

"Perhaps they went to the aid of the town?" Lyric offered, her voice peppered with hope, "Or perhaps they rode for help from a larger settlement?"

Luz turned to look back over her shoulder at the young Scribe. "There were no other travelers along the way. We would have seen them."

Lyric's lips turned down into a frown as she considered the implications.

She turned her gaze upward toward the Shrine above. The white stone gleamed and reflected the afternoon light. Normally, the historian would have been overjoyed by this sight, but a feeling of unease crept up her spine. It was unusually silent.

Closing her eyes, Lyric tried to listen all around her. There was nothing but her companions, the horses, the water, and the wind. Her notes did not show that the Verde Shrine was a silent shrine. The sounds of attendants and prayer should have been audible even from here.

There was nothing.

Opening her eyes, she noted Cortez had already taken out a looking glass and was scanning the area around the shrine. He, too, was clearly concerned about the absence of others from the area. After a moment's examination, he glanced at

Esperanza. A wordless exchange passed between them. In a graceful, cat-like motion, he effortlessly slid down from the wagon and landed on the ground without a sound. Taking up the long gun again, he took a knee and aimed at the large doors of the shrine above them.

Esperanza motioned for Lyric and Luz to exit the wagon quietly and follow her. Without saying a word, the trio of women slowly disembarked from the wagon. Lyric and Luz pulled out their pistols, while Esperanza seemed to emanate an aura of strength.

Slow and steady, the three moved up the hill as one, being careful not to let any surprises catch them off guard. Behind them, Jalin kept his sights on the door with his finger lightly tapping on the trigger guard of his weapon.

Finally reaching the top of the walkway, they stood before the massive pair of doors. There were no signs of distress or destruction. Everything was clean and well-maintained, as was expected. The complete absence of sound was eerie, leaving them feeling on edge. Esperanza gestured for her two companions to stand on either side of the door, their silhouettes visible in the afternoon light. She took a step forward, her hands slipping around the cold, metal handle of the door before giving it a sharp tug.

It did not budge.

Luz pulled the hammer back on her firearm.

Not giving up, Esperanza tried again.

Once more, the door failed to open. Esperanza narrowed her eyes as she ran her fingers over the latching mechanism, peering through the thin space between the two doors. It had been barred closed from the inside. Turning back to look at Cortez, she crossed her arms in front of her and tapped them together, then waited for his response.

From the foot of the trail, Jalin frowned. He raised his right hand off the trigger guard and made a slow cutting motion with his hand, then readied his finger on the trigger once again.

Esperanza nodded and turned to look at Luz. "Do not fire unless you see me act first," she said. Stepping up once more, she rapped on the door three times and took two steps back.

The silence was the only reply.

The quietness of the area was shattered by the steady sound of clicking, followed by a low hiss of air. The unfamiliar noise grew steadily louder until whatever was causing it was right on the other side of the door. Whatever it was, was directly opposite them. A loud scraping could be heard. Metal on stone. There was a loud THUMP against the door.

It shuddered.

Esperanza gestured that Luz and Lyric should hold fast.

The door shifted slightly. A heavy metal-clicking sound was heard. The massive doors shifted ever so slightly, almost as if they were breathing.

Someone or something was unbarring the door.

Esperanza closed her eyes and took a deep breath, readying herself for whatever monstrosity lay beyond the opening portal. She had done her best to prepare but was still overwhelmed when the doors finally opened.

Beyond the threshold sat a being in a strange-looking chair. A large metal frame held a red leather chair and elevated footrest. Extending from either side of the edges of the chair, where wheels might have been, appeared a series of metal gears in multiple leg-like designs. The chair hissed and wheezed from the pneumatic steam engine fixed to its back. A figure occupied the chair. The lower half of his face and nose were obscured by a mask and hoses that led to twin oxygen tanks. His chest appeared to be covered in armor. His right arm was encased in a bronze sleeve affixed to the arm of the chair. Ornate filigree was etched into its metal surface. Symbols of faith. His left hand was free and uncovered. Covering the figure's lap was an old knitted blanket. Worn and patched and threadbare in some areas, it was a stark contrast to the technology in which he sat.

The figure in the chair wheezed loudly, the expression in his eyes full of surprise, "You... you're not Brother Carson."

Lyric edged closer to the door to get a better look at its occupant. It was not armor that the figure was wearing. It was a respiratory plate. She recognized the work from the University Hospital. The markings and craftsmanship of the mechanism showed it was a product of the Mechanist Guild. Her eyes scanned the figure in the chair. He had clearly suffered either a massive injury to his chest, lungs, or both. His left hand told another story. While slightly faded with time, he bore the tattooed crest of Manos.

This person was an Inquisitor.

There was a hiss of air. She could see his chest rise slightly. His eyes scanned Esperanza as she stood before him. "Inquisitor of the Voice?" he asked.

Before anyone could reply, Lyric heard something moving quickly behind her. Her hand wrapped around the butt of her pistol. She turned to see Jalin sprinting up the hill. Stopping just short of Esperanza, he dropped to his knee and bowed his head. "Judex Stonebridge."

There was another hiss of air. "Jalin Cortez?" There was a slight chuckle. "Will Hil's wonder never cease?"

Pulling her gaze from a subservient Cortez, Esperanza turned back to the man in the chair, "Judex *Gale* Stonebridge, Hil's Sword of Faith, Inquisitor of the First?" she asked.

With a smile in his eyes, he managed a nod. "Retired, please - come in." Looking back to Cortez, "Jalin, do get up. We have much to talk about."

ALLEGIANCES

A place of peace and reflection.

This was the intention when each Shrine to Hil was fashioned. From the very beginning, when the first shovel was used to break the soil until the moment that the first candle flame was lit to illuminate the windows, a Shrine represented the land and the people it would serve.

The bricks of Casa Roja were baked from the warm terra cotta mud of its hills. The stained glass of La Playa Dorada was crafted from the golden sands of its beaches. Santuario Verde, the Green Sanctuary, was filled with plants and flowers, representative of the lush and vibrant life that filled the valley.

Lyric stood in the center of the Shrine and gazed around at its construction. It was a strange place. A combination of both old and new. Stonework that was almost three centuries old supported timbers that were less than a decade in age. The furnishings were likewise mixed and matched. Old benches, their edges worn smooth from generations of hands caressing their surface, sat next to metal chairs with ornate etchings, polished to perfection.

The wall at the front of the hall was decorated with an elaborate mosaic that depicted Hil's story and teachings. The gift of light and illumination to humankind and the world served as the central figure of the story. It was the primary lesson of the faith.

As her eyes traveled across the mosaic, the would-be historian in her noticed the subtle nuances of the pictures, searching for similarities and inaccuracies to the story she had heard throughout the Imperium. Her trained gaze settled on a set of figures to the left of the hall, illuminated by a soft amber light. Hil, their arms lowered and wide, palms open. Behind them, the light of the sun rose like a golden orb.

"Hil in Their resplendence," Lyric whispered. She stepped closer to examine the figures.

At Hil's right hand, a woman cloaked in a star-flecked dress shimmered in the light. Her head was raised toward the figure of Hil. Individual silver stars were painstakingly painted on the indigo mosaics that formed her dress, and fine strands of silver served as her hair.

"Lune of the night sky. Beloved of Hil."

She paused and took a step back to look at the figures there once more, then looked at Hil's outstretched left hand.

There was no figure on Hil's left.

Instead, in the place on the left, where Lune occupied on the right, there was simply a bare surface. The stonework

there had been worn to a soft, smooth surface from years
of being touched by hundreds of hands and lips.

The breath in Lyric's throat caught.

"Blessed Hanwi, may your heart find peace." The words
all but blurted from the scribe's lips, as she stood
dumbfounded before the figures.

Someone behind her cleared their throat.

Startled, Lyric quickly turned, almost falling into the
mosaic behind her. A strong hand suddenly reached out and
steadied her, squeezing her elbow softly before releasing
her.

"Inquisitor Cortez!"

The lanky Inquisitor watched the Scribe with an expression
of surprise and respect, a stark contrast to his usually
disdainful gaze. He drew his attention away from her, and his
gaze fell upon the mosaic figures before them both. Then he
lowered his head in reverence before turning to her.

"Faith rarely finds purchase in the hearts of historians," he
said. His deep voice reverberated off the aged stones that
surrounded them. "In my experience."

Lyric regarded Cortez for a moment. In the time they
had spent on the road together, the Inquisitor had shared
little in the way of casual conversation with her. His attitude
towards her was only one of having to fulfill the assignment
and nothing else. Mostly, she felt he looked upon her
as a nuisance, but he was determined to keep her safe,
regardless.

"The tale surrounding the Heart of Hanwi has always held
a specific interest for me."

"Ah," came the simple reply. "Your interest is purely scholarly then. I shall leave you to your musings." He inclined his head and stepped away.

Lyric watched as he moved to turn from her. "Do you have an opinion?" she blurted. "On Hanwi…"

Hesitating for a second, the Inquisitor bowed his head slightly before glancing back in Lyric's direction over his shoulder. "I do. But I do not believe it is one that you would care to hear."

The hiss and click of the steam-powered chair crawler broke their exchange. Lyric noticed as Jalin's unusually relaxed figure suddenly stiffened up into his usual rigid posture.

"Judex," Cortez bowed his head in the sound's direction and the man in the crawling chair that approached them both.

The man in the chair waved the fingers of his left hand in Jalin's direction. The forced oxygen hissed as it pumped life-giving air into his mask. At his side walked Inquisitor Boyorquez.

A half a step behind and to the left. Lyric noted. This was clearly a man of some importance, even in his proclaimed retirement.

Air wheezed into and out of the Judex's lungs, "I see… you have found… our Honoring of Hil… and the Lady Lune."

Lyric's eyes lit up at the unspoken invitation to comment from the man in the chair.

"Indeed!" she exclaimed. Her youthful voice was filled with delight, making the room feel alive. "The University does not have many remaining images of the Sky Sisters. I have only ever read of them in the Library. This is the first time that I have seen Them depicted in person. They are extraordinary." Lyric turned to face the mosaic once more. "The empty place to Hil's left. That is where Hanwi would be if I am correct?"

The Judex wheezed and nodded. "It is."

"And the smooth stonework... indicative of those who have come to beg for forgiveness?"

Another wheeze, "Or mercy."

The young historian whirled back to engage the man in the crawling chair. "Did they come here then?" she asked. She spoke in a hush, her voice barely audible, but her entire body trembled with anticipation. "The Moon Cursed? Did they come here?"

A round of wheezing suddenly overtook the Judex. Jalin stepped to his side quickly, and Esperanza reached forward to steady the chair.

"You are irritating him with your prattle." Cortez snapped, the bite returning to his tone.

Lyric frowned.

From his chair, Judex Gale Stonebridge waved his fingers once more and shook his head.

"He's laughing," Esperanza said quietly.

"What?"

"He's laughing, Cortez, he's fine."

Jalin's brow furrowed, and he took a step back. He nodded. "Of course."

"It's fine. It's fine." Stonebridge wheezed. He turned bloodshot eyes to Lyric. "Your passion... is commendable... young lady." he managed. Each wheeze was accompanied by a measured handful of words. "It is possible... yes." he nodded. "The Reach... to the West... drove... the last of the Moon Cursed... from its borders... a decade ago. It is possible... they came here, yes."

Jalin's body tensed at the comment, and a look of anger crossed his face.

"But I have not seen them." Stonebridge continued.

"Then Moon Cursed did not..." Lyric's voice trailed away.

"Murder the entire town of Paraíso Verde?" Jalin finished her thought. His lips were pulled tight in an unhappy, wrinkled frown. He slowly lifted his hand and massaged the back of his neck as he pondered. "It would have to have been more than one." His eyes slid to Esperanza.

"It would also explain why they collected all the bodies." She answered and then turned to look at Lyric. "We cannot rule them out."

Lyric cast her eyes to the ground in thought at the response. "I see."

The mechanical chair Stonebridge was sitting in clicked and wheezed in the silence as the three Inquisitors gave the young Historian a moment of silence to grapple with her inner turmoil.

The Judex spent an hour questioning them, asking them to recollect their observations and account for what had happened in the town. From an outsider's perspective, his inquiry was overly analytical and too meticulous to yield meaningful results. He seemed mired in the minutiae. Questions centered on the most minor of details, from the smells in the air and the color of blood to the consistency of the mud and in which direction they entered the town from. He forced Jalin to produce the chunk of flesh that was discovered and insisted on examining it himself. Lyric watched silently as Cortez's features shifted from admiration to hesitation, to something akin to shame, at every question and second guess. She felt that same exacting demeanor turned in her direction. It was like she was back at the University and being tested by an instructor, and each of her answers was found wanting.

It seemed apparent that Stonebridge suspected what they were dealing with, but refused to commit to the declaration. It was a diagnosis by exclusion. She could catch hints of the picture he was drawing, and it did not bode well for any of them.

Reaching into the small pocket that was part of the mechanized chair, Stonebridge pulled out a well-worn smoking pipe and leaned back as far as the chair would let him. It was carved from wood and animal horn, nothing fancy but a favored item. Despite his inability to partake, he held the object in his rough, calloused hand as he stared at the scene before him.

"We received... a strange report... a few days ago... from a trio of villages... to the northeast," he wheezed. "A rash of attacks... that bore more intelligence... than animal cunning. The local Peacekeeper... requested official intervention... as they believed it was something... unnatural. I sent a courier... yesterday. But I believe... Hil has answered... my request for help... already."

Jalin inclined his head toward the seated man. "We are here to serve..."

Esperanza cut him off, holding up a cautioning hand. "Of course, we have to root out the darkness, but how prepared are we, Inquisitor Cortez?"

Jalin scowled at her, but the Judex lightly raised his fingers as if to say 'Hold'.

"She brings up... a valid point... You have... no retinue... no gear... and only... the robes on your back... with weapons... that you brought with you... You do not know... the nature... of the trouble... or how deep... the darkness may go... You are walking... into a dangerous situation... blind." He paused and locked his gaze on Jalin. "Stupidly blind. Have you ... such a desire ... to add your name ... to the Martyr's Wall... that you are willing... to throw your life away ... on a whim ... and a rumor?" His tone bore a sense of disappointment, like a father to a child.

Jalin's face flushed. He stared at the older man and replied in a crisp, respectful tone, "Sir, no, sir." As he stood up to attention, his voice was filled with admiration as he continued, "I am the Hand that swiftly cuts the Darkness. I am the Hand that will bear both the Light of Hope and the Fire of Judgement. My Life is to serve the will of Hil, to ensure the Light of Providence, and to protect the devout. I fear not the denizens of Shadow or their corruptible servants. As the Light touches the land, so too will Hil's Judgement befall those that seek to fester in the abyss. By Fire, by Blade, and by my Hand - my Watch is Eternal, and the Hunt is Unending. This I Swear."

Lyric thought she saw a glimmer of a smile appear on the old Judex's face, hidden under his mask. He recognized the words that Jalin was reciting now.

Each servant of Hil swore an Oath of Service to the Divine when they took up the mantle of Inquisitor. No matter the role one played, or the position filled, the basic tenants of the oath were the same: ensure the Light of Hil brought all evil and corruption to heel. Judge the wicked and preserve the innocent. Those called to serve as the Voice of Hil were administers of faith, healers, and defenders of the innocent. They had the sacred task of looking after the sick, and Hil's special gifts were made known through their care.

Esperanza was one of these.

However, those Inquisitors that were invested in the position of Hand were of a different calling. They had a martial duty to fulfill, which had physical and spiritual requirements that differed from their companions. Illuminated by Hil's light, they were determined to vanquish darkness, wherever it may have been found. The duty of the Hand was demanding and without yield. They were formidable warriors and unparalleled protectors.

But there was a danger in the passion that moved the hearts of those who called themselves Hands of Hil. A danger that made eyes blind to some truths and steeled hearts against compassion for others. Where one must do whatever is needed to protect humanity, there was value in that grit and steel. A Hand that flinched or paused at the sight of a weeping figure, could well be taken down by a Lady in White, and their charges lost to twisted works of darkness. But the price of that steel was often debated.

The words Jalin spoke now were the Creed of the Hand.

"Well, then... boy... what is your plan... for all of this?" the Judex asked. Lyric could hear it in his tone, over the whir and wheeze of the machinery. This was a test.

That fact was clearly not lost on Jalin, either. He took a deep breath, and his eyes fixed on a place on the ceiling above them. He raised his right hand and tugged gently on the short whiskers of his chin, as if in thought.

"To start off," he said, "I will need to go over the report and try to get as much information as I can before we can go any further." He then paused and moved his arm behind his back, firmly holding it with his other hand. He paced.

"We will need to chart our routes to the said investigation." He glanced at Luz, the Guild representative, who was leaning against the wall across the room. "I may need your eyes on those."

Luz nodded silently in agreement.

"If one lacks a retinue, an Inquisitor may grant a temporary station of Acolyte to any Shrine Laymen or willing citizen of the Imperium."

The Judex agreed.

"It is also within an Inquisitor's authority to commandeer any necessary equipment." He paused then and gestured to the surrounding building. "The Shrine should not just be a place of worship but should also be equipped with the tools and equipment to protect it from harm. A weapons locker." He glanced at the main in the chair. "As the retired Judex, I cannot imagine you would have permitted such a storehouse to become barren," Jalin said with an odd smile, then asked the question they had all been wondering since their arrival, "Where are those that tend to the Shrine?"

"Not here," said the old man simply.

Jalin pursed his lips in frustration at the unhelpful response.

"What do you mean not here? This is a Shrine of Hil. There should at least be a half..." He stopped himself and looked back over his shoulders toward the direction of the town.

"Mother Nessa... departed this morning... to attend to a woman... not long for this world. She... and her two attendants... have not returned." Stonebridge wheezed his responses. "I expected them... when you knocked... If the attack is... as you have said... anyone out there... alive... is waiting for help... there is no one available," the Judex said.

Jalin made a sour face and glanced at Luz and Lyric.

Lyric blinked, surprised to be included suddenly in the conversation. Her eyes met Jalin's. There was an unasked question lurking behind his dark eyes. *Can I count on you?* She inhaled a shaky breath. This was her Prueba, her time of truth. Her behavior during this mission would decide her status and position when she got back to the University. There were two Inquisitors and a Judex all with eyes fixed upon her, awaiting the decision that would shape the rest of her life.

"I will accompany you, Inquisitor Cortez," she answered.

Jalin nodded satisfactorily.

"However," she quickly added. Her palms grew slick with sweat as she hesitated, trying to decide what to say.

Jalin's eyes narrowed as he watched her, waiting for her to go on.

" I do so as a Servant of the Throne. My Oath of Service prohibits serving others, including the Divine." She swallowed hard and met Jalin's cool gaze once more. Her heart pounded in her chest, "None May Serve Two Masters."

Jalin's lips twisted into a scowl and his eyes darkened. "Fine," was all he said in response and turned away.

Esperanza smiled at the young woman's reply.

Lyric's eyes fell to the floor, and she felt a tightness in her chest as she took a shuddering breath. She could not refuse the request for her abilities, yet her role required her loyalty to the Imperator was a priority over her loyalty to the Divine. Without a Peacekeeper, it would be her job to make sure local laws and customs were considered before any action was taken. She knew already that Jalin Cortez disliked being questioned. She dreaded what might come next.

Jalin turned his chill stare at Luz. "And you?"

"I can lend you the use of the Guild maps in the wagon. If they will help?"

Jalin nodded in thanks. "They will."

Stonebridges's characteristic wheeze interjected, "I have need... of the Guild... in this."

"Of course." Luz agreed.

"We need... to send word... to the locals... and bring them here...where they... will be safe." The Judex added.

"A reasonable request, certainly. The Guild is at your disposal, Judex Stonebridge."

"Retired." He insisted.

"Retired." She agreed.

"You say you... have... a wagon?"

"We were making a delivery run. Yes."

Stonebridge gave a nod. "Will the Guild... permit these representatives... use of their transport... to investigate... this situation?" he paused and took several deep breaths.

The conversation paused.

"Judex Stonebridge?" Esperanza asked. She took a step closer to his chair.

He waved her off. "Too much talking... not enough... action." He smiled through his mask.

"Of course," the healer replied.

"Did I see a mule around the back when we came up to the front?" Luz asked.

Stonebridge nodded.

"Not my favorite animal, but you are many and I am only one person. You need the wagon. I don't." She turned her gaze to rest on the Judex. "I will need your eyes on my maps to point out where I need to go."

"And compare them against maps here, so we know where we are headed," Jalin added.

"In the classroom... across the courtyard... you will find... what you need."

Luz glanced at the Scribe. "Wax, you're with me. Let's go find some maps!"

Lyric's previously sullen face lit up once more at the promise of dusty books and wrinkled paper. She followed the Guild Courier out the door.

SANTUARIO

Lyric marveled at the natural beauty of the area woven into the design of the courtyard and buildings. As with all Shrines, the architects and designers had taken great pains to make the place of worship one that felt like it belonged to the landscape here. An open-air courtyard separated the building of the main shrine from several smaller outbuildings. A kitchen and small dining hall with seating for only twenty spoke of a few attendants and visitors that often took meals here. Its doors hung open. Simple bench seating was visible within.

The courtyard itself was designed for both comforts and socialization. Spacious benches where conversation or reading could take place occupied the verdant area. A small stream flowed through the center of the courtyard, no doubt water from the Rio Vide, incorporated into the design. The water was pure and clear, adding a visual reminder of the life-giving essence the valley depended on to those who visited the Shrine. A large stone obelisk, the color of dark sand, rose from the center of the courtyard. Sunflowers grew around its base.

The stream ran up to the base of the obelisk and then split into two branches to encompass it, forming a small island upon which the obelisk sat, rejoining into a single rivulet once more on the other side. That rivulet wandered out of the courtyard and down the side of the hill atop which the shrine was built.

The center of the obelisk was hollowed out and its surface was covered in carvings dedicated to Hil. If one stood on one side, they could see through one side of the obelisk to the other. A deep niche was carved into the center of this hollow. A glint from the contents within the niche caught the eye of the Scribe as she passed by on the way to the classroom on the opposite side of the courtyard.

Lyric paused and turned her attention to the monument.

Squinting, her eyes focused on a multicolored stone seated in the niche.

"An El EmGee!" she gasped and stepped quickly toward the stone. The breadth of the small stream made it impossible for her to step to the other side of the small island where the obelisk sat. She scoured around for something she could use as a bridge.

Nothing existed.

Luz turned at Lyric's gasp, hand on the butt of her pistol. She calmed when she noticed it was only the historian who had stumbled upon another oddity.

"What is... El EmGee?" Luz asked as she approached.

In the center of the niche sat a multi-hued stone that appeared to be growing out of the center of the obelisk. Its vibrant colors caught the ambient light surrounding them, making it appear to glow. Vivid yellows and golds shifted to an almost iridescent metallic purple. Looking at the stone from a different angle yielded facets of green and blue.

It seemed almost alive.

"Hrmm?" Lyric mused. "Oh… uh… The remnants of a lost language. It was the only thing scholars could make out where this item was concerned, so they applied the name to the object. It's not pronounceable by humans," she replied in a very clinical tone. Her eyes surveyed the shore once more, earnestly trying to see if she could cross. Dejected, she shoved her hands into her pockets and leaned forward to see the object better.

"Legends say that humans were not the first creations. There were others who came before us. There is some debate, both scholarly and philosophical, on exactly where humanity was ranked in the order of creation. We were certainly among those first created… but not THE first… this…" She marveled once more at the strange item carefully nestled in the niche. "This belonged to those who came before us," she whispered almost reverently. "The current theory is that the El EmGee promotes vitality to the surrounding area. While this has not been proven … areas that house one seem to be more verdant." She examined the obelisk and the rivulet. "This was clearly designed to pull water from Rio Vide, wash it past the El EmGee and then deposit it back into the river itself," the Scribe said. She wanted to reach out and touch it, to feel that fabled pulse of life. Instead, she shoved her hands deeper into her pockets.

"I wonder if someone found it here... in the Valley and built this to house it, or maybe it was brought here by one of the Viajero."

Luz shot her an alarmed look. "The Harbingers?" She took a quick step away from the area and made a sign to warn off evil.

The spell of curiosity and natural beauty was broken by those words. Lyric sighed and glanced back at her companion. "Please tell me you don't believe that?"

The look on Luz's face was a mixture of embarrassment and disdain. "Wherever those creatures have been seen, death follows. This is a fact! When those... things... come up from the Southern border, it is always a bad omen." The courier made the warding sign once more.

Lyric sighed and ran her hands through her hair. She wanted to sit Luz down and explain to her how she was incorrect. Yes, the Viajero were a rare sight this far North. Yes, their appearances often coincided with misfortune. However, the Viajero were not the cause. Convincing the Courier of this, on word alone, was not something that Lyric was prepared for. She wanted to reach for one of a dozen books and show her the historical truth behind the appearances and disappearances of the Viajero... the Travelers. But she was hundreds of miles away from her Library and her reference materials. She could almost see University Librarian Dierdre shaking her head and rolling her eyes as Lyric disappeared back into the stacks to dig out another tome of history, intent on combatting the superstition with which the Imperium insisted draping itself. She missed Dierdre and her infectious laugh. The Librarian could have recited the title, chapter and page of the reference that would have settled the matter. Lyric had only just graduated from Clerk to Scribe. Perhaps one day she would have half as much information at her own disposal.

She closed her eyes, and took a breath, then turned away from the El EmGee and back to Luz. "Let's get those maps so we can do our jobs."

Luz bowed her head and whirled away from the strange object in the middle of the courtyard, and Lyric begrudgingly accompanied her.

Esperanza observed from the doorway to the Shrine as Lyric and Luz stopped for a moment in the courtyard. She wiped her hands with a rag as she watched, then tucked it into her belt. The words of the two women drifted across the space to Esperanza and fell upon her listening ears. She understood Luz's hesitation at the mention of The Harbingers. They were, as their epithet implied, messengers. Unlike the couriers of The Guild, however, the appearance of Viajero always heralded ill fortune. Whether they preceded it or proceeded it, Esperanza did not know. But that Lyric Wax did not hesitate to name them in conjunction with an

El EmGee was problematic. How could an El EmGee... a sacred item ascribed to the Primeras have ever been in the possession of a Viajero? The idea itself seemed repellant.

Her assumptions were likely fueled by her youthful curiosity. Or perhaps the Imperial University was encouraging a line of thought in its Scribes that would benefit from Hil's oversight. She tucked the observation away as something to discuss at a later date, then turned and walked back into the heart of the Shrine.

Simple wooden benches and seats filled the circular room that housed the main Shrine of Hil. A large stained glass mandala occupied the dome-shaped ceiling. Warm reds, yellows, and orange glass formed the ornate sunburst shape above. In the center of the mandala was the sigil of Hil. The light from the sun shone on the sunburst and illuminated the room. Hil's sigil had been inscribed, so that same light projected the sigil onto the dais below. It was a masterful combination of artistry, engineering, and faith.

Esperanza loved the simplicity of the room. The stained glass above was its only ornamentation. Hil's grace stared down from the heavens on them all. There were no precious metals that adorned the setting. No gold filigree or expensive oil lamps decorated the Shrine. No extravagant inlay inset on the benches. They were crafted from hardwood, worn dark with the touch of hands whose blood and sweat tended the surrounding lands. Here and there she could see the telltale signs of where bored children had once sat, digging tiny lines into the wood with their fingernails. A rite of passage, she well remembered herself. Families congregated to hear words and tales, unions were sanctified, and babes were introduced to Hil's light here.

It was a place of quiet meditation, where one could commune with the divine. Esperanza closed her eyes and took a deep breath, filling herself with what should have been Hil's presence. She frowned. The presence was still here but muted. Sandalwood and cinnamon were the favored scents of Hil. Their warm, spicey scents often filled the sacred spaces. The aroma was here, but distant, almost like a memory. Services had not taken place recently.

She glanced around the room. Eight niches sat at the points of the sunburst. The eight-pointed star of Hil. In each niche sat a candle and incense. Every candle was dark. How long had the others been gone? Perhaps the plan had been to hold services at daybreak upon their return.

The Judex was in no condition to tend the dais and make offerings, and the lights needed tending.

Walking over to a small alcove along the wall, Esperanza located a small metal container that held the incense and a few spare candles. Smiling, she retrieved the small white candle and held it near her face. She closed her eyes and called on the warmth of Hil that rested within her. Reaching into herself, she said a quiet prayer, followed by words of power. Soon the candle flicked to life with fire. She smiled and inclined her head in respect and honor. Giving another silent word of thanks, she took up a handful of incense and then walked clockwise around the room, starting with the Easternmost point. She paused at each niche and used her candle to light the wick of the candle there. As the light glimmered, she ignited a small rondel of charcoal in the niche and placed the incense on top. Scented smoke was pulled through a carved airhole in the back of the niche, carrying the sacred smoke, and Esperanza's prayers upwards toward the sigil of Hil.

Soon, the warm and comforting scent of sandalwood and cinnamon filled the space once more. Satisfied, Esperanza walked to the dais and placed the candle in the center. Kneeling, she bowed her head and began the prayers she would need to steel her soul against the darkness on the horizon.

Hil had faith in her. She would not fail Them.

SECRETS

J alin stepped lightly down the hallway next to his mentor. The only sound was the whirling gears on Stonebridge's crawling chair. They had left the company of the rest of the retinue to inspect the weapons locker in the belly of the Shrine. Maintenance and upkeep of the arsenal was the duty of the Hands of Hil. The Shrine had been tended to by healers and scholars. Not a single warrior of the Faith was present. Stonebridge, while ailing and retired, maintained what he could. He confessed he had been preparing to request a representative of the Manos to be assigned shortly before this occurrence. Mother Nessa and Brother Carson had not agreed to his reasoning. The Valley had been at peace for over a decade.

When we become complacent in our preparedness, evil prevails. We must always be prepared.

Jalin glanced up at the ceiling and the walls. They were clean. At least the acolytes kept up their duties on that measure. He dreaded to see the condition of the arsenal.

Stonebridge was in no condition to polish and oil blades, or keep rust off of firearms. He remembered seeing a stream outside.

If the powder got damp...

They stopped before an unmarked door. Jalin looked down at Stonebridge, who reached into a pocket of the chair and produced a set of keys.

Holding up one, "Use this one... only turn left... ninety degrees. Precisely. Wait for the sound... of a click. Once it you hear it... a full turn... clockwise will unlock." He wheezed.

"Combination lock?" Jalin asked.

"Simple. But still... effective," came the response. Jalin took the key and inserted it as he was instructed. Turning the key, he waited. He heard several ticking sounds until a loud click resounded. Peering back at his mentor, the Judex nodded and so Jalin rotated the key completely and heard the door unlock. He waited a moment and then heard another, heavier mechanical sound.

He pushed the door open.

Behind the door was a room no bigger than many dormitory rooms at the Academy. Jalin glanced right and saw a series of gears build into the wall alongside the doorframe. His eyes traced the locking mechanism. A small glass vial filled with green liquid was set into one of the gear cogs.

"Poison?"

Stonebridge shook his head. "Knockout gas... Nessa did not... allow... poison... on the grounds."

Jalin pursed his lips and nodded and turned his focus back to the contents of the room.

Sets of tall, closed cabinets lined the walls. Along the back of the room sat a few stands that held hardened leather armor pieces. A plain cotton sheet had been tossed over one of these in the corner. Jalin glanced back at his mentor, who simply gave him a nod.

Jalin crossed the room to pull the dust sheet off of the stand in the back of the room and revealed an ornate set of decorated half-plate. Dents, chips, and mended breaks covered the armor. This was practical armor. Field armor. It was not intended for decoration or frivolous parades. This was the Judex's personal set that protected him in the field and also bore his seals of office.

Jalin recognized this suit. He had seen his mentor wade through dangers and nameless horrors while wearing it. Looking back at Stonebridge, he saw the Judex had been staring at it as well.

Slowly, the old man pulled his eyes from the memories on the stand. "Cover it up," he said, then shifted and motioned toward the cabinets.

With a flick of his wrist, Jalin floated the sheet back over the Judex's field armor, hiding it once more from view.

The first set of cabinets contained a half dozen long guns, some pistols, assorted maintenance tools, and plenty of ammunition. The second cabinet contained an assortment of short swords and knives, along with sheaths and leather strapping. Jalin smiled to himself. While he required little, save the extra ammunition, it would be enough to supply the witch and the scribe.

"If I were you... I would not... be smiling," Gale whispered.

Jalin closed his eyes and felt his body tense up. He had been waiting for this.

"Turn around... and look at me..." his mentor said.

Jalin turned and stood at attention. His eyes met Gale's for a moment, then looked down.

"By the gods... I said... look... at... me! Here! In my eyes!" Gale roared through his mask.

Not willing to let reluctance show, Jalin's gaze met his mentor's. His mentor's expression was different, far different from what he had remembered. His eyes were tired. There was no anger or cold steel there. He was just tired.

"What happened... back there?" he demanded. "Snapping... at a civilian?... Open disdain for... your second? My gods man... I raised you... better than this!"

The last words hit Jalin in the chest like a sledgehammer. For a moment, he was in the training room at Sanctuary. His knuckles were bruised and bloodied while another boy was on the floor, crying. Back then, it was the Judex who stood tall, looking down at Jalin, who had beaten down a fellow Ward. The reason did not matter. None of it mattered because he struck someone outside of sparring. He expected to be dismissed right there and then.

Instead, the Judex challenged him. If he wanted to pick fights with those who were bigger than him, why didn't he start at the top? Without hesitation, he charged the Judex only to find himself smashed to the ground with his arm locked, and pain shooting through his body. His pulse pounding in his ears along with his rage prevented him from hearing the Judex's words as he addressed the other Wards.

All he could remember was pain, and then a pop as he felt his arm wrench out of the socket. The pain had been so much that he passed out.

Waking up in the infirmary, he saw the Judex sitting across from him. The eyes were not angry or filled with disappointment; they were just tired.

Like now.

Those same tired eyes stared at him from the mechanized chair, "I told you... a long time ago son... you can have... all the physical skill... in the world... but you need... to use... your head. Make your mind... as sharp... as the blade you carry. I know... the last seven years... have been... rough on you. Hell... it would be... rough on anyone... in your position. But you... still came through it." Despite the tired eyes, Jalin could see a rare smile from behind the mask. "You've been... on fight... and survive mode... for so long... that you have... forgotten basic diplomacy. I need you... to be... sharper in mind... not just stronger... There is more... to our Mission... than just... being the hand... that wields the blade. The Voice... may speak for us... but they... do not... lead... us!" The fire in his words triggered a gagging cough. Jalin stepped forward but was stopped when Gale raised his hand to hold.

Forcing deep breaths, he looked back up at Jalin's face of concern, "I'm fine... son. It may appear... that I've been relegated... to the pasture... but trust me... Hil placed me here... for a reason."

"Then whose plan was that?" Jalin asked as he motioned to the chair and respiratory plate.

For a moment, the Judex's expression was a mix of anger, shame, and then tired acceptance. "The cost of hubris." He paused then and gestured to the door.

Jalin crossed the room and closed it, careful not to allow the locking mechanism to engage once more. He grabbed a weapons locker and dragged it across the room to sit before the Judex and his crawler chair.

"I'm listening."

"Two years ago... the Cult of Bone... began building itself up... south of the Imperium proper... They were... ill-prepared for us... or so we thought." Gale shook his head, "Lives were lost... and I was... too engaged... with the fervor of the fight... I had taken wounds... but didn't realize... the level of maliciousness... the cult... was capable of... Their weapons... were coated with Carasin."

Jalin's face went red with both anger and disgust. Carasin was a poison derived from the bones of the dead. Specifically, those who died of disease or infection. Those that came into contact with the substance lived a life wracked in pain as their internal organs suffered from necrosis. There was no cure for it. Often, it was better to put someone out of their misery than let them linger in such agony.

His mentor refused to die.

"A few favors... were called in... and I underwent... the knife... several times... in order to be... outfitted with this... Shortly after... the notice was put out... that I wished... to step down... and the Lord Inquisitor... named Esteban Crowne... as my successor... No mention... of the infection...

or surgeries... just a quiet... retirement." His expression was that of disgust at the phrase.

It made sense why the leadership would want to keep his mentor around as the man was a storehouse of knowledge, but in this state, it just seemed... cruel. Jalin knew the older man would have wanted to die in the field fighting the darkness, making that ultimate sacrifice. Yet he was denied even that.

"I'm sorry sir, I..."

"No, son... no... I don't want... apologies... I want you... to do better...I want you to... be... better. You are my... legacy... to the Order... Do not... waste your time... on me...There are... greater plans...for me... I know this... and I believe... in my faith... to guide me."

Jalin met the eyes of his mentor and nodded. "As you wish."

Gail nodded in reply. "Good. Now. Are you... taking your... prescriptions?" he asked.

Jalin's chin dropped to his chest, and he reached for the cuff on his left arm. He deftly loosened its fitting and pulled the material up, revealing his forearm. Four jagged scars trailed down the meat of his arm. They were dark, fleshy things with black centers and red edges.

"There has been no change. It's been over a year." He said.

"You must remain... vigilant."

"Claws, not teeth." He rolled the shirt sleeve back down and fastened it closed once more. "I am not infected."

"Hanwi's curse... is insidious... the goddess..."

"Will die by my blade if I ever find her." Jalin snapped and stood.

The old Judex nodded in his chair. Forcing himself to sit a bit taller he continued, "I charge you... with leading... this investigation... Supply your team... and watch out for them... Do not berate... Encourage... be observant... Wax is naïve... she is... a Servant... of the Imperium. She will act... in defense... of the Imperium. If she dies... or worse... it will... come back on you... because the Imperium... will require its... reparations... She is your priority..."

"What about Boyorquez?" Jalin asked.

"Be fair... their kind... wear the mercy... of Hil... on their hypocritical faces... while wielding power... that should not... be theirs. Use the witch... where possible... If she must be sacrificed... for the greater good... so be it," he said.

GREEN GREEN GRASS

The wooden table shook as the armor landed on it with a rattle and thunk. Lyric jumped at the sudden and unexpected noise, her eyes ripped from the maps she had been exploring.

"Protection." Jalin's deep voice said. His deep brown eyes met Lyric's. "The Voca and I both have our own, but you will be in the field, and it will be important you are properly outfitted as well."

"I... understand," Lyric replied. She rolled the map up, tucked it into a hardened case, and stood to face Jalin. Scribes were seldom issued armor unless they were to be part of an Inquisitorial retinue. They were taught the basics of how to wear the items that might save their lives but rarely had cause to don it.

She looked down at the items on the table. A banded leather back and breastplate, hardened leather vambraces for her forearms, and a pair of matching greaves to cover her legs. The leather had been dyed red and was ornamented with Hil's golden sun sigil.

"The choices available were limited." Jalin offered.

Lyric nodded and looked back up at Jalin with a gentle smile. "The effort is appreciated, Inquisitor. Thank you."

"It is no effort. You are my charge and responsibility. The Imperial Court would look poorly on both myself and Boyorquez if something were to befall one of their Scribes on her Prueba. Your search for truth begins here, Ms. Wax. It should not end here as well." He looked away from Lyric then and gestured to Esperanza. "Boyorquez will assist you in dressing."

"Of course."

Jalin's eyes searched the courtyard. He looked to Esperanza, who had stepped forward to help Lyric gear up. She answered without being asked.

"Luz departed while you were with Judex Stonebridge. She took what she needed and the mule and headed north. The Guild does not dally, and she had a substantial distance to cover before dark." She tugged on the straps, securing the ill-fitting armor as best as she could to Lyric's frame. She scowled and looked up at Jalin. "This was the best you could find for her?"

"Ten years of peace limited my options," Jalin replied.

Esperanza pursed her lips and tugged once more, pulling the banded mail as close as she could. It was too big. There was nothing more that could be done.

"Can you move in it?" She asked the young woman.

Lyric twisted back and forth and bent forward slightly. She shrugged in response.

"It will have to do then." Esperanza sighed.

Across from them, Jalin had been cinching on his own field gear. He slid into a sectioned metal cuirass and checked the straps on his scoring blade. Without a word, Esperanza finished with Lyric and then walked to Jalin and checked his straps and fittings, then helped him slide into his leather duster. There was a silent and almost ritualistic pattern between them as the two Inquisitors put on their arms and armor. No quips. No jibes. No sneers or insults were exchanged between them. In those silent moments, they were Manos and Voca, the Hand and Voice of Hil, and Lyric could see why they were chosen to serve.

Lyric examined the map cases again and stowed them away safely into her satchel. She strapped on the holster for the pistol she had been given. Words were her weapons, not these.

"You'll want a blade," Jalin commented.

Lyric shook her head. "No. I... I am terrible with them."

"And you'll wish for one if you find yourself trapped somewhere."

Esperanza rested a gentle hand on Lyric's arm. "Listen to him in this. He is not wrong."

A feeling of tightness wrapped itself around Lyric's chest for a moment, accompanied by a wave of nausea. She was not a field Scribe. She was a Clerk in the Library. The worst injury she'd ever had was a paper cut from the stacks that required stitches. Maybe she could just stay here with the

Judex and interview him until they returned. Certainly, that would be enough.

She closed her eyes, took a deep breath, and leaned into Esperanza for a moment. The Healer held her up and looked over the top of her head at Jalin, who pursed his lips in thought.

"My search begins here. It does not end here." Lyric whispered.

Esperanza leaned in. "What was that, child?" she asked.

Lyric took a deep breath and swallowed hard. She forced herself to stand unaided and straightened her shoulders. She opened her eyes and smiled at Esperanza. Then she turned to look back at Inquisitor Cortez, who stood watching the two of them.

"My search for truth begins here. It does not end here." She paraphrased the words that Jalin had spoken to her.

The left corner of Jalin's mouth twitched upward at her response.

"And so it does."

There was a misconception about mules, that Guild members learned early - they were not stubborn, they were ridiculously smart. It was this inherent intelligence that often made them difficult to handle, as they had a mind of their own and both the will and strength to enforce it. The mule from the Shrine required more prodding than Luz would have liked. It had clearly been used as a pack animal and was not used to trail riding.

It had been an hour and a half since she left the Shrine. Glancing back over her shoulder, the Shrine appeared as a white pebble balanced on a larger green one. She peered skyward and then used her hands to count how far the sun was from the horizon.

Two hours. She had two hours to make it to a secure destination. Though, from what she recalled of Paraíso Verde, a locked and bolted door may not be enough.

She reached forward and patted the neck of the mule. Despite its lack of training, the animal would still be of value to her. Many of them hated the smell of blood. Miners used canaries to detect poison gas in their mines. Guild drivers often had mules in their train to detect blood. They were used to help protect a traveling group and offer an early alert to some of the more undesirable inhabitants that still roamed the Imperium.

Something had murdered the people of Paraíso Verde, and Luz could use all the warning she could get. Her left hand slid to check the saddle ring and the firearm there as her eyes scanned the horizon.

The maps from the Shrine showed that the path to the first farm was through a sea of green. Tall grass. Luz observed the land was suitable for cattle grazing, though there were none in sight.

The wild grasses here grew almost a yard tall. The warm afternoon breeze danced across the field. The grass swayed back and forth, like the waves of some strange ocean. Luz had grown up on the northern coast. The grass there rarely grew in this abundance. The colder weather produced squat and stunted greenery. Not like here. This valley was full of life and vitality.

Luz's thoughts drifted back to that strange stone the Scribe had talked about in the Shrine. Was it truly responsible for this beauty? And what of its odd origins? The Scribe had discounted her beliefs regarding the involvement of the Harbingers. That was because she was an academic and did not know of the world outside her Library and her books. Those that spent their time in books and buildings never saw the world for what it was ... and what it could be. The creatures that dwelled to the south were unnatural. The stories of the Harbingers cemented that fact. They were no better than the other monsters out there.

Shaking her head from the memory, she focused ahead through the sea of green. In the distance, she could see a few black specks on the horizon. Buildings. Her initial destination. She might coax the mule into a trot or a gallop, but for how long? She was also unfamiliar with this trail, and could not afford to have the animal falter and fall.

Two hours of sunlight.

The farm was about an hour away.

She had time.

A gust of wind pushed gently on her back, and for a moment everything seemed serene. Despite the horror that happened in the town, the surrounding land seemed untouched. Pure. Pristine. What did the Guild say about Paraíso Verde? At peace for a decade. She felt a bit of calm contentment. Take a deep breath and relaxed into the saddle.

Her serenity was shattered as the mule let out a deep bray and stopped dead in its tracks.

"What's the issue?" Luz sat forward and looked around.

Then the scent hit her. Something foul and unwashed. Glancing back at the sea of grass, she watched as it swayed back and forth in tandem with the wind. She saw nothing out of the ordinary.

The mule brayed once more.

Luz braced and forced herself up, to stand in the stirrups and get a better view.

Waves and waves of green grass surrounded her.

The breeze faded, taking the foul smell with it. A stillness settled over them both.

Luz settled herself back into the saddle when the breeze started again. The smell was stronger than before. Looking behind her, reached for her pistol.

It was too late.

THE GREAT GATE

Mathis was one of the mining villages that had sent word to Santuario Verde several days earlier. It was north of Paraíso Verde and nestled into the Vargas Mountain range. Lyric and the others had come from Valle Espino in the East, through the Central Pass of the Mountain Range. They had seen and heard no commotion along their way here and they passed no one on the road back.

The Vargas Mountains were a towering display of nature. It was said that if you were to travel the length of the range, you could experience everything nature could offer. Decades before the Great Accords that united The Reach with the Imperium, the Vargas Range separated the two kingdoms as a natural border. The passes in the northern and central parts of the range merged the two kingdoms as one.

The Western side of the Pass was home to The Reach. The wealthiest Kingdom in the Imperium. The Eastern side of the Pass housed two other kingdoms, the University, and the Imperial Palace. The Pass itself was guarded on both the

East and West entrances. Imperial Guard and detachments from the Temple manned the Pass, helping ensure safe travel between locations. Anyone seeking access to either The Reach or the remaining Imperial Lands would have to navigate the Vargas. That meant going over the mountains, controlling the Pass, going around them at the far north, or daring the lands to the South, hoping to find another passage.

To reach their destination, they had to backtrack the way they had come.

Lyric sat next to Esperanza on the buckboard seat of the wagon, reviewing the maps of the area. Luz had marked Guild weigh stations on it for them before departing in the opposite direction to send word to the farmers in the area. If they needed help or supplies, they might find them there.

"The three townships that sent word asking for aid are all mining villages," Lyric commented.

"Far enough away from each other and anyone else that trouble might go unnoticed for some time," Esperanza commented.

Lyric's brow knit together, and she stared at the map in thought. "Perhaps."

"Do we know the order the missives were received in?" Jalin called out. He sat in the back of the wagon, toward the rear, watching the road and the horizon behind them. His long gun rested across his lap.

Lyric frowned and grabbed her notebook. She skimmed through the pages there and reviewed her notes. She shook her head. "The Judex was uncertain. Mother Nessa did not tell him which order they came in, only that they had arrived. He was given the impression they all arrived at the same time." She looked up from her notes and back at Jalin. "Perhaps they all arrived at the same time because that was when the Courier's route brought them?"

"Are they on the inside or the outside of the Great Gate?" Jalin asked.

Lyric cast her eyes once more on the map, her finger tracing the various roads and pathways until her finger came to rest on the spot marking the small mining community if Mathis. Her heart beat a little faster.

"All three use the access point on the IN-side of the West Gate." She looked up at Esperanza and then back at Jalin. "This isn't contained."

Jalin nodded once and turned his eyes back to the horizon. Esperanza snapped the reins on the horses and brought them into a steady gallop as they traveled toward the looming mountain range.

The sun was setting as they neared the Central Pass. Roads diverged from the Great Gates, leading to various townships, villages, and outposts. A settlement had grown up around the Central Pass over the years. Travelers stopped here before either continuing through the Pass to the East or going onward to their destination in the West. The Guild maintained several way stations here with Runners and Couriers servicing locations in the settlement and beyond. Hil's Faithful kept a miniscule Temple and Salon Guard were sent from the Imperium. This was a crucial travel nexus and was heavily guarded.

They were no longer the only ones on the road. An assorted mix of travelers made their way both to and from the Great Gate by mount and wagon. As Lyric observed the many travelers on the road, she fervently wished that none of them would go back the way they came.

"Do we warn them?" she asked.

"And tell them what?" Jalin replied. "Paraíso Verde has been destroyed by an unknown assailant? Lock your doors and windows?"

Lyric bristled at Jalin's tone. People were in danger. They needed to know what was happening. As if in response to her unspoken fury, Esperanza lay a warm and gentle hand on the Scribe's arm.

"Until we know what is afoot, it would only create more fear than these people already live with."

"But we could ask for help…"

Jalin turned to look over at her. "When you were choosing your assignment, were there any other Inquisitors scheduled to come through the Pass this month? A scheduled retinue change? Armament delivery?"

Lyric lowered her eyes and stared at her hands. Jalin knew the answer to those questions as easily as she did. This was the only assignment through the Central Pass. They could ask for aid from the Temple, but they would have no Manos or Voca available to join them. The location here was a Temple in name only. A place to offer prayer and ask for blessings. The Salon Guard were needed here to protect the Great Gates and the people here.

"We ARE the help, Ms. Wax," Jalin said flatly.

"On the way back, once we know if the occurrences are linked... we send word then," Esperanza offered.

Lyric nodded in uneasy acceptance, then rolled the maps up and tucked them away once more.

Looking up and around, she noted many of those traveling were merchants or Guild Couriers. Distant conversations floated on the air. Too many and too varied to make out anything of importance. All the travelers wore the same weathered look that spoke of too many hours on the open road. These were the people who were the lifeblood of the Imperium. Their actions kept trade and communication alive and prospering. Lyric's thoughts drifted to Luz, the Guild driver who had brought her from the Eastern side of the Imperium and through this Pass only a few days prior. Despite her differences with the courier's superstitious beliefs, she hoped she was well on her way to warning the other farms.

Looking behind her, she watched as the horizon shifted from bright orange to a deeper hazy red. A blood-colored sky. Yesterday, she would have gazed at it with fascination. Now she could feel her stomach churn. Taking a deep breath, she felt eyes upon her. Cortez was watching her as he sat in the rear of the wagon. His dark discerning eyes watched her face and then glanced skyward before settling on her once more.

He nodded once. It was a knowing gesture, as if to say 'I understand'. Returning the nod, she pulled her attention back to the road ahead of them.

The road ahead was lit by torches placed at measured intervals along the sides. An hour before sunset, the Salon Guard would begin lighting these. Darkness was as much an enemy as the creatures that made their homes within it. The lights provided a muted measure of safety for those traveling.

All the lights eventually led the way to the Great Central Gate. Two massive towers acted as hinges on the large double doors made of wood and steel. The partial military installation was manned by both the Salon Guard, Gate Staff, and the Runners. The huge doors were routinely sealed twice a day in anticipation of a potential prohibition. Their travel through the Great Gate was without incident.

A Runner came alongside their wagon and asked Esperanza about their destination and their business.

She had replied, "Mathis for an investigation."

The runner gave her and the others a quick glance, jotted some notes, and made his way to the next traveler. Lyric recognized the man as a fellow Scribe from the Crest of the Imperium tattooed on the right side of his neck. She knew the information taken down would be recorded and sent to the Imperial Archive for final cataloging.

"Pen at the ready," she said to the Runner.

The Runner paused in step and looked at Lyric with a slight smile. "See the World as it sees you," he said and gave a nod of his head before heading to the next traveler.

"What was that about?" Jalin asked.

"A professional courtesy. It will also ensure that the record of our trip is given a bit more attention. If anything happens,

I would rather our respective keepers be aware of where we went sooner rather than a month from now," she said.

"Smart," was his only reply as he turned a critical eye on the various runners and watched them keep pace with their charges.

Lyric allowed herself a small smile and looked at Esperanza. The other Inquisitor raised her eyebrows and nodded her head. Civility was one thing, but stand-alone praise and not a back-handed compliment from Cortez was surprising.

After passing through the gate, they followed the signs that directed them off the main road and onto the larger uphill path. Jalin pulled an oil lantern that bore a polished back panel out of a wooden box in the back of the wagon. Lighting it, he attached it to a pole and passed it forward to Esperanza. She inserted the pole with its lantern into the bench seat between the driver and passenger. The reflected light illuminated their path enough to give Esperanza and their horses another fifteen feet of visibility. Like the road leading to the Great Gate, the mountain road also had lanterns along its path. However, unlike the Great Gate, this road lacked dedicated Guards to keep them lit and several had gone out.

Part of Lyric wanted to stop and light them for other travelers, but she decided not to mention it. The Inquisitors were on an investigation, and while a deed, it would only waste precious time. She could include the observation in the missive they would send on the way back.

From the crags of the mountain pass, in the darkness above them, several shapes watched the lone wagon as it traveled along the road. They were dressed in torn and dirty clothing, stained with dried blood. Hoarse whispers and hisses passed between them. These were silenced by a single hooded figure. She stood, eyes glinting in the moonlight. A sense of raggedy neatness about the figure. She dropped the hood and her dirty hair rustled in the wind. She turned to the group and spoke in a broken voice.

"We... leave... now."

Scaling the mountainside with unnatural grace, the group followed her into the darkness and headed back toward the Great Gate.

Mathis

The road to Mathis was uneventful and quiet. As the light from the sky faded and they ascended into the mountains, shadows took their place around them and the temperature dropped. Above them, Lune's lonely light shone her half-hooded silvery face down from the heavens.

Lyric shivered in the cold next to Esperanza. She had packed for the warmth of the lowlands, not the mountains. She was thankful for the Voca's presence. The Gifts of Hil allowed her to remain warm when it would otherwise be cold. She shared that heat as best as she could with the young Scribe at her side.

A warm glow in the distance told them all that they were approaching the settlement.

Esperanza gazed into the distance at the approaching lights.

"How many people live in Mathis?" She asked.

The lantern was not enough to allow Lyric to consult her notes. She had to recall what she remembered reading.

"Maybe ten families? Only 50 total residents. It's the smallest of the three. Why?" She followed Esperanza's gaze. The light from the approaching settlement was too great to be from lanterns and forges.

"Because someone clearly enjoys burning buildings," Esperanza replied. "Jalin…"

"I see it," came the reply. The distinctive sound of a long gun being checked echoed afterward.

Esperanza urged the horses to move faster along the road and towards the town on fire. The closer they got, they could see efforts being made to control the fire. They could also see groups of people carrying lanterns and weapons. They were patrolling the area. Whatever had happened was still happening.

The lone wagon rushing toward the town caught the attention of the people, who turned their attention to its approach. They pointed and shouted and gathered as a mob, ready to intercept it. The Inquisitors were met by an assorted group, covered in dirt, soot, coal, and blood. Their expressions ran the gamut from desperation and fear to elation at seeing the newcomers.

Esperanza pulled the wagon to a stop and handed off the reins to Lyric, then stood on the buckboard seat. She raised her right hand and wrapped the fingers of her left around the emblem of Hil at her throat. Her hand glowed, then erupted into holy fire. The reddish-yellow flames lit up the area brighter than any torch. The power of the divine quelled the group into silence. Lyric sensed the emotions transforming around her. Fear gave way to relief and even hope.

"I am Inquisitor Boyorquez and this is Inquisitor Cortez. We are the light and salvation of Hil. Who speaks for Mathis?"

One woman turned to a younger man, "Get the doctor, tell her the Inquisitors are here!" The younger man nodded his head and sped off back to the village.

"My name is Norma Cain. I'm one of the Dig Overseers. Believe me when I say that we are thankful for your attendance, but it's been almost two months since we've sent word," the woman said.

Esperanza furrowed her brow and turned to look at Jalin. Before she could say anything, Jalin's face twitched and his nose wrinkled.

"Graverot," turning his attention back to the crowd, "How many of them?"

The putrid scent wafted forward on the breeze and soon enveloped the group. Lyric covered her nose and mouth and forced herself not to retch.

Norma answered, "We've put down at least three, but there seem to be more. We don't understand where they are coming from. What's worse is that their bites have been infectious!"

"Wait! What are you...," Jalin started.

He was interrupted by a roar of yells and screams filling the air. The crowd turned their attention away from the newcomers and back toward the town. One group had encircled something. Norma and her people peeled away from the Inquisitors and marched back toward the light of the burning buildings.

Without waiting for the order, Lyric flicked the reins, and the horses moved forward toward the growing crowd.

Jalin hopped out of the wagon and walked alongside them. With a flex of his arm, locked his silvered scoring blade into place. The smell of decay and rot grew stronger as he made his way into the crowd.

In the center of the group stood a large man. He towered above anyone else gathered around. One of his booted feet was planted in the center of the chest of some creature. His other foot stood on the forearm of this rotting monstrosity. In his hands, he gripped a pitchfork that had pierced the creature's throat, pinning it to the ground. The creature's other arm and its legs were being held down by other men. The creature was held in place by the big man's strength. Turning his head to Jalin, he fixed his eyes on the blade and armor.

"Inquisitor I take it?"

"You the doctor?" Jalin asked as he kept his eyes on the creature.

"He is not," said a voice from the crowd. A tired-looking woman in a blood-stained apron made her way through the crowd. "Mr. Carstein had the misfortune of arriving a few days ago. But his help has been a godsend. I'm Pilar Miracle, a local physician and, unfortunately, de facto speaker for Mathis."

"It's Finn, Dr. Miracle, just Finn," the man said.

"Doctor Miracle?" said Jalin with a slightly bemused tone.

The doctor's tired eyes hardened and she shot him a look that said two words, 'Try it'.

Rather than pursue the challenge, Jalin asked, "How are you destroying them?"

"Holding them down, taking off their head, and setting their remains on fire," she said simply. "Fire kills most things, Inquisitor. Hil taught us that." She looked at the large man with the pitchfork. "Finn, if you would allow the Inquisitor to do the honors?"

Nodding his head, Finn looked at Jalin.

"On your mark."

Jalin shifted and readied the blow. They could not afford to miss.

"Mark!" he shouted.

As one, Finn pulled the pitchfork out of the creature's throat as Jalin brought his scoring blade down. The creature convulsed and endeavored to bite Finn's boot before the silvered surface of the scoring blade punctured deeply into its flesh and lopped off its head from its neck.

They all stepped back as Esperanza stepped forward. Still holding the fiery light in her hand, she spoke a prayer and let the ball of fire fall from her hand to engulf the creature's body.

The light of the flame glowed fiercely but did not produce a true measure of heat. In fact, the faintest sense of warmth radiated as the fire quickly devoured the creature's body. Nothing of it remained, not even ash to mark its passing.

They spent the next few hours helping to contain the fires and ensure everyone was safe. The families who had been displaced found refuge with other families, or in the main hall of the building that served as the Salon. Although the building was not large, there was enough space for makeshift beds, and the hearth provided warmth for all. Jalin aided the villagers by setting up a rotating watch for the rest of the evening. Esperanza helped Dr. Miracle tend to the injured. Thankfully, the numbers were few.

Lyric stood on the porch of the Doctor's office, watching the villagers. She wrapped her arms around her body and shifted from foot to foot to keep warm.

"It's probably warmer inside." A gruff voice offered.

She turned and saw the huge shadow of Finn approaching. He was carrying something in his hands.

He stepped up onto the wooden porch. It creaked beneath his weight.

"Coffee?" he offered and extended a cup to her.

"Thank you!" Lyric replied and accepted the warm beverage. She wrapped her hands around the heated ceramic mug and blew across the surface.

"They had drinking chocolate earlier, but I think the kids drank it all." He turned to stand next to her and stared out at the night.

"Oh, that's all right. I'm sure they needed it more than I do." She sipped the dark, bitter liquid and welcomed its warmth as it blossomed in the pit of her stomach. "Thank you for the gesture."

The big man's shoulders rose and fell in a simple shrug. "If we don't take care of each other out here, no one else will."

"I suppose you are right."

Finn sipped his coffee and continued to watch the village and the night sky.

"Imperial Scribe?" he asked after a moment.

Lyric nodded.

"Assigned to the retinue?"

She shook her head, "Prueba."

Finn's eyebrows rose at that. His grey-blue eyes glanced over at the small woman standing next to him. "You seemed older."

Lyric sipped her coffee once more. "I turned twenty this past Spring."

Finn pursed his lips and nodded quietly. "I didn't mean to pry."

Lyric shook her head and looked up at the big man, "It's fine. Really. This has been the most normal conversation I've had in the past week. It's appreciated."

"Had to come all the way up a mountainside and deal with the unmentionable for a normal conversation ... that .. is ... something," Finn mused. A grin tugged at the corners of his mouth.

Lyric allowed herself to smile over the rim of her cup, and she nodded. "The Inquisitors are..."

"Inquisitorial?" Finn offered.

"Mmm. Indeed."

"Well, I am glad I could bring some levity to your quest for truth, then." He sipped his coffee and watched the shadows. Peeling away from the darkness, the lean figure of Inquisitor Cortez strode in their direction. "May you have as pleasant an evening as fate and duty will allow." He said to her, then stepped away. He inclined his head politely to Cortez as he passed him on the way.

"Inquisitor."

Cortez gave Finn a sharp nod and stepped up onto the porch.

"Did he need something?" Jalin asked.

"He brought me something warm," Lyric replied.

Jalin frowned in thought for a moment. "Ah." then, "It is probably warmer inside, Miss Wax. You should go inside and sit by the fire."

Lyric nodded.

"Boyorquez?" Jalin asked.

"Inside with the Doctor. They were finishing up. I needed some air."

Jalin nodded then and positioned himself next to the young woman, his arms folded across his chest, vigilantly examining the area. He shifted his weight and then lifted his left hand to tug on the short hair of his beard and roll the end of his mustache.

"That creature..." Lyric began.

"Yes?"

"Do you know what it was?"

"Not yet," he replied.

"It did not seem capable…"

"Of cognitive thought? No. I agree." His dark eyes drifted to the cup in her hands. "If you have finished your reprieve, our answers probably lie inside." He gestured to the door.

Lyric stared at Jalin's hand for a moment and then took a deep breath. Gulping down the last dregs of her coffee, she readied herself for what lay beyond.

"I'm ready."

QUESTIONS AND ANSWERS

A potbelly stove warmed the offices the tired group gathered in. A copper kettle boiled water atop its flat surface. The doctor had used the boiled water for both sterilizing instruments and pouring into another pot filled with an herbal concoction. An herbal tea she'd given to two patients in the back room. With Esperanza's help, they had bandaged and mended almost everyone. The tea was a simple painkiller to help them sleep.

Esperanza had pulled a chair close to the stove for Lyric to sit in and found a warm blanket for the young woman. She was bundled up now, and trying not to fall asleep.

Across from her stood Jalin. His hands folded behind his back as he stared at a map of the area that was tacked on the wall. Multi-colored pins were pushed into it in different areas. He scrutinized the map and stretched his neck.

"These pins..."

"Each mark where an incident was reported over the past two months." Dr. Miracle replied. She untied her soiled medical apron and tossed it into a pile of laundry in the corner.

"Do you know the origin?" Esperanza asked.

The doctor shook her head. "Not specifically, no. It could be Biruji, the town up the mountainside, or could have been further north in Tayler. Kay Stone, the Peacekeeper, headed up to Tayler a couple of days ago. She wanted to ensure there were no more of those creatures lurking about."

Jalin nodded. "And the locals assumed the attacks were Daerrog- related?" he asked.

"We have enough of them up here. It was easy enough to assume." She shifted some things on the surface of the stove and set a pot of coffee to boil. "Tayler's a new dig site. Travelers come and go up here looking for a bit of money for a week or two. People don't show up, and it's just assumed they went back down the hill. Finding two workers turn up dead was a shock. According to the local healer, it was hard to determine the cause of death given the state of the bodies. It wasn't until the third body was found that a local in Tayler reported seeing something move in the darkness around the outskirts of the mine shaft. That was when the Daerrogs were considered the source of the issue."

Jalin took out a small notebook from the inside of this jacket and began jotting things down.

Lyric stirred from her bundle, "Forgive me doctor, but I'm not familiar with Daerrogs. What are they? Are they some sort of animal?"

Pilar reached over to a modest bookshelf on the wall and thumbed through its pages.

"Daerrog. From the Canis Araneae. Spider Wolves… not to be confused with wolf spiders, which are much smaller, and far less deadly."

She handed the book to Lyric. Displayed on the pages were several artist renderings of a horrific creature the size of a dog, but with 6 legs and pitch-black fur. Eight red eyes stared out of its forehead from the page of the book.

"They are pack animals that live in the Vargas. Nocturnal. No one knows their origins, or if they do, no one has ever shared that information."

Lyric stared at the creature for a moment and shuddered. She handed the book back.

"Thank you."

Pilar accepted the book back and tucked it back into the shelf. "They see humans as nothing more than challenging prey."

"So, when did that theory change?" Esperanza asked, "That the issue was not the local wildlife?"

Pilar responded bleakly, "When they discovered three Daerrogs dead in Biruji."

Jalin's face sharpened. "Killed in a similar fashion to the people?"

Pilar nodded her head. "Torn apart. Normally a few dead Daerrogs mean fewer issues for us, but according to the report," she pulled a folder out and handed it to Jalin, who leafed through it. "The ferocity with which they were torn apart was... unsettling. It was at that point where things escalated."

"The bodies that were buried... they came back as ghouls and began causing issues?" Jalin asked as he paged through the file.

Pilar nodded her head, "Yes, but we knew ghouls were not capable of taking down one, much less three Daerrogs. They aren't organized enough." The coffee on the stove was boiling. Pilar walked back to the stove and poured herself a cup. She gestured to the contents with an open invitation and continued, "Two of the ghouls killed a single person. The ghouls were a father and an adult son who were first found. Their victim was an old man that they attacked in his sleep, the man's father-in-law. He had been bedridden for the last few years. The wife was forced to shoot the corpses of her husband and son as they were feeding on her father." Pilar rubbed the bridge of her nose. "The next night, no one could find her - the wife, Dolores Gouveia. She was gone."

"That poor woman!" Lyric exclaimed.

Pilar nodded in agreement. "The bodies of the three men were set to a pyre that night. The foreman didn't want to take any chances. A courier was sent from Tayler to the Gate for a Guild runner to contact the shrine in Paraíso Verde. With two ghouls, Peacekeeper Stone figured it was best to let your lot know since you have a better way to deal with this sort of thing. Dispatch a priest or someone to consecrate the burial soil or whatever needed executing. After a few weeks, we still had no word. Things got quiet. We thought it was an isolated incident. Then hell broke loose in Biruji."

"What happened in Biruji?" Jalin asked.

"Biruji is newer than Mathis, but also larger. New dig, more opportunities for expansion. More people come up the hill, hoping to get rich." She made her way to her desk and finally sat. She rubbed her eyes a moment, then drank from her cup before continuing.

"When things went bad in Tayler, Stone sent word back here to Deputy Robie. She was going to stay in Tayler for a week. She wanted to find the Gouveia woman. A few days after that, Stone received a message in Tayler that a plague had broken out in Biruji. She sent a runner back here to alert Robie. Robie took a few volunteers and some building supplies and headed out to Biruji. My guess was that Stone went up to Biruji to work with the healer there and stop the illness from spreading. She must have asked Robie to head up and fence off the road," said the doctor.

"Quarantine?" Jalin asked.

"My best guess," Pilar replied.

"What was the nature of the illness?" Esperanza asked.

"Fever," Pilar said. She leaned over and opened a drawer in her desk. She took out another set of folders and handed them off to Esperanza, who read through them. "Victims experience an intense fever, inability to hold down any food, and ultimately death. 100% mortality rate. You catch this thing, you die."

Jalin and Esperanza exchanged guarded looks.

"What I say now is conjecture and speculation based only on these reports. I have inspected none of the victims, nor the assailants. No one is certain who the first victim was. But each of the reports that Stone sent back confirms that each victim who died came back more... savage. Feral is the term Stone used. They attacked others. Anyone who was attacked contracted the illness. That was how the infection spread." She paused and looked at both Inquisitors. "I don't believe this is a medical emergency. I think it's something else."

"You think Stone failed and may be dead, or worse?" Jalin asked.

Pilar paused at the directness of the question. Then her shoulders slumped. "We've had three ghouls make their way here. Actual ghouls. You don't work out here in the mining communities and not be able to recognize them for what they are." She sighed. "I don't believe Stone's efforts to quarantine the infection are working, and it's been several days since the last report from either her or Deputy Robie. If the infection is coming... it's going to come through here."

Lyric looked to both Inquisitors. Jalin chewed the inside of his cheek in thought. Esperanza's eyes were closed, her head nodding as if going through her own stores of knowledge.

Before Lyric could ask, Jalin spoke. "What I beheaded out there was a ghoul. They are corpses inhabited by desperate souls that have already gone mad. They are slow, sluggish, and ill-coordinated because the body they've inhabited is rotting. The consumption of flesh - living or dead - helps ensure it keeps going, but they don't possess the strength or cunning to take down a man. A bedridden elderly person... perhaps. But an adult should be able to fend them off. Even a powerful malevolent spirit could only be as strong or as fast as the body that it inhabits. Daerrogs hunt living creatures.

Just like their smaller counterparts, they feed on the flesh and blood of the living. A walking corpse holds no interest for them, and they are fast enough to avoid being brought down by ghouls. Whatever this is, we need to go see for ourselves. With any luck, we can find your Peacekeeper and help re-establish the line of quarantine."

The bunkhouse was warm, and a welcome refuge from the day's troubles. The large main room served as a mess hall and gathering area for the miners without homes in the area. Rooms to the right and left of the mess hall offered a place to sleep and store one's personal gear. The rooms to the right of the main door were barracks-style bunk beds. The rooms to the left held two beds each and were assigned to the foremen and overseers of the dig. Norma Cain shifted some people around for the evening to give Esperanza and Lyric one room while Jalin propped himself up in a chair in the main room, with his long gun across his lap and his hat over his face.

Lyric tried to find comfort in the lumpy bed and the four solid walls around them. It was the first bit of security she had felt since they entered Paraíso Verde.

Was this the reality for those living outside the walled cities? She lay on her back and stared at the ceiling. *Was this what the Corpse Wars had left behind?*

Lyric had enjoyed a simple life inside the walled Capital of Roca Aguila. Her family was not wealthy, but her father was part of the Mechanist Guild. When her mother died, her father's connections secured a place for her in the Library.

It was modest.

It was simple.

It was safe.

She started as a Page, running missives from department to department. Then was promoted to Runner, taking messages from the Library to other businesses and offices in the City. She'd spent a summer interning with Professor Henner, learning hand languages, so she could communicate with those who communicated differently or were non-hearing. He was developing an entire language that Runners could use to send messages across the city with nothing more than their hands and a spyglass. It was brilliant.

Everyone has a voice. You have to listen with more than your ears. He used to tell her.

She could have remained with the Runner-Corps. The work was reliable. Information carriers were always in demand in the City. Sometimes Runners would even have the chance to be assigned to other cities, or stationed at places like the Great Gate. Occasionally, The Guild itself would recruit from the Runner-Corps to supply its ranks of Drivers outside the city walls.

Then she met Dierdre.

A Librarian.

She was the keeper of history and information. In that single meeting, Lyric's entire life changed. The missives she carried now were manuscripts or texts that held stories of the Imperium, or older. She wasn't transporting grain orders from one merchant to another, or class rosters for administration, she was transporting history.

Deirdre was impressed with her dedication, and when it came time to appoint Clerks to the Library Office, she invited Lyric to join. Now she wasn't running information, she was reading it and recording it. Simple things at first, keeping track of Runner routes, and who carried which manuscripts to which Historians. She was assigned to a specific researcher, and she managed their notes and research files. She checked out their research materials and ensured they were brought back and shelved. She even got to sit in on their classes and meetings. She gleaned a great deal without ever enrolling in a single class... officially.

She'd pushed off her Prueba as long as she could, just so she could maintain her position. But with the passage of her twentieth birthday, she had no choice. She would never be seen as an adult until she completed it. Deirdre would not let it stand.

You've hidden here long enough. There is an entire world out there. You have to see it, so you can decide who you want to be.

She made Lyric a deal. Choose an assignment, be promoted to Scribe and Deirdre would help her get her Imperial Mark. When she returned, she would get her red quill added to it and could take her choice of appointments. But she HAD to go. No more delays.

Lyric placed her hand on her neck over her tattooed Mark.
She curled up and rolled on her side, facing the wall.
It was supposed to be a supply run.

Esperanza sat on the bed across from Lyric with her eyes closed. She counted as she inhaled and again as she exhaled. With every breath in, she infused herself with focus, and with every breath out, exhaled distraction, anger, and fear.

She had to maintain composure and focus. Within her, bubbled a font of Divine energy. She had used that blessing this evening to bring light into the darkness, to heal the injured, and to purge the world of that creature in the center of town. Whenever Esperanza allowed Hil's Gifts to flow through her, joy and elation filled her. Being one with the Divine, for even the briefest of moments, was a feeling that had no comparison, nor words to do it justice. It would be easy to lose oneself in that reverie. To surrender to the power completely.

But that exchange came with a cost. The mortal body was not designed to channel Divine power. The joy of that brief union also brought exhaustion as the energy tore through her physical form. Too many who were blessed with the Gifts of the Divine lost themselves to that joy and allowed their bodies to become nothing more than husks.

The Inquisition's ranks were not filled with these privileged few, for a reason. Many failed to survive their training.

A sound at the door pulled her from her thoughts.

Tap-Tap-Scratch-Tap-Tap.

She frowned and unfolded herself from the bed. Careful not to wake the Scribe in the bed opposite her. She padded across the room and unlatched the door, then pulled it open.

Cortez peered inside the room from the hallway.

"Problema?" Esperanza asked in a light whisper.

"Is she asleep?" said Jalin.

"Mostly... I think. What is it?" she asked.

Jalin gestured for Esperanza to step out into the hallway. She cracked the door open and slid out.

Jalin looked down the hall and back into the main room. Both were empty. They were the only people up and about. He looked back at Esperanza.

"This is not the work of ghouls." He whispered.

Esperanza narrowed her eyes.

"Ghouls are slow, and lack reasoning. They are ghosts piloting a decaying corpse. The reports all show that while they seem to match the feral nature of ghouls, the afflicted attack with speed." He let Esperanza consider his words.

"Ghouls aren't fast." She confirmed.

Jalin shook his head. "No. This is something else. In the morning, I will send a message out to the Great Gate and have it delivered to Santuario Verde. Judex Stonebridge needs to know."

Esperanza looked over her shoulder and back at the room. "Do we send the girl away as well?"

Jalin considered a moment and then shook his head. "No. It's too dangerous."

"More dangerous than where we are going?"

"Sending her with a Runner, even a Guild Driver, down the mountain with known Daerrog and Ghoul activity, plus some other unknown?"

Esperanza nodded. "At least with us, she will have a fighting chance."

"Precisely."

"What do you need from me?" she asked.

"Talk to Hil. There is an ill wind blowing tonight, and we will need Their Light," he said.

A measure of silence passed between them. Then Esperanza replied, "I shall, good night, Cortez."

"Same," he said and departed into the night.

SERVANT OF THE THRONE

"**W**E DON'T CARE WHO YOU ARE! THIS AREA IS OFF LIMITS, TURN BACK AROUND!"

Lyric jerked awake, eyes wide. She shook the sleep fog from her mind and scanned the area. Her heart pounded in her head and in her chest. She was in the wagon once more. Esperanza was beside her. Jalin was behind them both. He was standing, long gun at the ready.

She remembered they were in the Vargas. They'd departed Mathis shortly before sunrise. There was a chill in the air. She blinked twice and sat up.

A fence-like barrier stretched across the road before them. Several women and men, armed with picks, sledgehammers, and shovels, stood guard at the barrier.

"Nice of you to join us," Jalin quipped to Lyric.

"Thank you for guarding my sleep, Inquisitor." She replied without missing a beat.

Jalin checked the breech of his firearm in response. His eyes narrowed on the group standing before them.

"Take your wagon and your missionaries and go back home!" a man shouted at them.

Esperanza's face clouded with disdain. "I am no missionary!" she replied in a flustered tone.

Lyric pulled her red curls back and secured them into a messy bun with a quill pen. She scanned the group once more. A glint of morning sunlight reflected off of the metal at the throat of one miner. It was an Imperial Mark. He owed allegiance to someone. Or used to.

She patted the backboard between the two Inquisitors, "Let me deal with this."

Both looked at Lyric with a sense of shock but said nothing.

Hopping out of the wagon, Lyric raised her hands and walked toward the barrier. She fixed her eyes on the man wearing the mark. "Excuse me, sir, are you in charge here?"

The group exchanged concerned glances.

"Listen, lady, we are under orders of the Peacekeeper of this region. Their authority exceeds all others, so get your ass back in the wagon and turn the hell around!" said the man with the mark. He rested a heavy-looking sledgehammer over his shoulder.

Unphased, Lyric continued to walk forward and began tugging at the fabric of her neckline. "Do you see this tattoo, sir?"

"I don't give a f..." he started but paused as his eyes narrowed at the image on her neck. "I'm sorry, but..."

"Do you SEE Imperator's Crest, sir?" she said as she continued to walk forward.

"Yes ma'am," the big man said.

"What am I sir?" she asked. She was ten feet away from the barrier, and all eyes were on her. Some of them had slightly paled.

"You are a Servant of the Imperium," he said. The loud irritation had been drained from his voice and had been replaced by a sense of concern.

"Article 12, of the Codex Deber, states that a Servant of the Throne bears the responsibility of its citizenry in overseeing the duties of those tasked with the safety of the people such as the Peacekeepers. Now tell me, sir, what is your name?" Lyric demanded.

"Orban, Miguel Orban," the big man stuttered.

"Now Mr. Orban," she said, "I am bearing RIGHTFUL WITNESS, as Scribe, to the duties of the Inquisition of Hil in concerns to this area's infestation of ghouls. You will let us through now, and you will tell me where we can find Deputy Robie or Peacekeeper Stone. If you continue to prevent us from our duties, I will report your interference upon my return." She held her gaze on him. It was a cold and unflinching stare.

He finally lowered his gaze.

Clearing his throat loudly, "Open up the barrier now! Imperium business is allowed." Turning back to Lyric, "The deputy is up in Tayler, but Stone is still holding the barrier down outside of Biruji."

"Your assistance will be remembered, Mr. Orban," Lyric said as she turned around. "Four ghouls were killed last night in Mathis. You need to do better, Mr. Orban...for all our sakes."

The rough barrier was opened up just as Lyric swung herself back into the wagon. Urging the horses forward, the wagon made its way down the road.

Once the barrier was no longer in sight, Jalin looked down at Lyric. "What is Article 12 of the Codex Deber?"

Lyric blushed slightly. "Instructions on the proper handling and storage of agricultural records. I figured no one out here would know what that was, but as my instructor used to say, speak with clarity and confidence, and none will know the better."

"So, you lied?" Jalin asked.

"Yes sir," Lyric said.

"Good job," he said simply.

"Why were they not going to let us pass initially?" Lyric asked.

"On official investigations, Inquisitors travel with a retinue and not in a borrowed Guild wagon," Esperanza said. "They had been requesting help for the past two months, and two individuals in a wagon are not the image they had imagined bringing help. We were clearly suspect."

Lyric nodded. "That makes sense."

Esperanza gave a slight smirk, "Where to... oh, Rightful Witness?"

"The deputy is in Tayler, but Stone is still in Biruji," she said.

"Biruji," Jalin noted, "We push on. Our answers are with Stone in Biruji."

The road to Biruji was well-maintained.

Both Tayler and Biruji were new dig sites. New dig sites often attracted more people to the area. That meant roads needed to be maintained. No matter how well-maintained, mountain roads were still susceptible to rock and mudslides. Miners were better equipped to deal with these obstacles than many, and often had the tools needed at the ready. A road that might have been blocked for a week or more otherwise could be cleared in a day if they all pulled together.

A well-used and maintained road still presented danger from sharp cliff faces and blind turns. A rider or cart could drop over the edge and fall to their death into the darkness-filled chasm below. Once in a while, someone would build guard rails along the more perilous areas of the road; but more often than not, it was the skill of the driver that determined successful navigation of these areas.

Esperanza carefully coaxed the horses around the curve of the road. A recent mudslide had narrowed the road here. If she took the turn too sharply, the wheels would lock, but not sharp enough and the driver's side wheels would catch air and the wagon would topple. Lyric and Jalin walked behind the wagon.

"Watch the area," he told Lyric as he stepped up to the back of the wagon to check the angle. "You are good back here!" he called out to Esperanza.

She nodded and clucked at the horses. "Easy. Easy. Step. Step." The wagon inched forward. The horses snorted and chuffed and pulled.

Rocks slid away from the back edge of the driver's side wheel as it slowly advanced.

"Step. Step." Esperanza coaxed. The wagon slowly pulled around the curve and cleared the edge.

"Clear!" Jalin called to her.

Esperanza nodded and allowed the horses to pull the wagon forward another ten feet before stopping and allowing Jalin and Lyric back in.

"Impressive driving!" Lyric smiled as she climbed back up onto the buckboard seat next to Esperanza.

Esperanza nodded politely. "My family has been Guild Drivers for many generations."

Lyric's eyebrows rose. "And you are not because… "

Esperanza touched the golden sun emblem at her throat. "I was called to a higher purpose."

Jalin scoffed behind them as he settled back into his position.

Esperanza's mouth drew into a tight line at the unspoken comment and turned to face the road. Lyric reached over and placed her gloved hand over hers and looked into the Voca's eyes.

"I am thankful for your skills," she offered.

The Voca nodded and patted Lyric's hand, then snapped the reins and they resumed their journey.

They made their way along the road, and through passes carved into the rocky earth. By the time they reached the outskirts of Biruji, the sun was high in the sky.

"Slow us down, but be at the ready," Jalin cautioned. As before, another barrier presented itself before them. Unlike the barrier at Tayler, long guns pointed directly at them as they approached.

"YOU WILL STOP AND IDENTIFY YOURSELVES!" shouted someone across the way.

This time it was Jalin who stood. "The Inquisition of Hil, as requested by Mathis. We are here to find Peacekeeper Stone."

A tall woman with a beaten hat stood up and lowered her rifle. "Kind of late to the party, aren't you Inquisitors?"

"Two months of lost messages will do that," Cortez said back. "Are we allowed to have a normal conversation, or should we continue shouting at one another?"

The woman motioned to the others with her, and the firearms were withdrawn. Approaching the wagon, she removed her hat and revealed a mop of shaggy blonde hair. "I'm Kay Stone, Peacekeeper for the Great Central Gate. Timing or not, I'm glad someone got the message."

Esperanza gave the woman a nod. "I am Inquisitor Boyorquez, this is Inquisitor Cortez. Also, with us is Imperial Scribe Wax. Doctor Miracle debriefed as best as she could. However, you should know that at least four ghouls have made it as far as Mathis. The locals stopped them, but they got past your barrier at Tayler. We were told the creatures here in Biruji were infectious, so we made our way here as fast as we could."

"Jimmi, take the Inquisitor's wagon to the stable and make sure their horses are taken care of," Stone said to one man. Turning back to the visitors, "You will want to see for yourself. I am not sure what they are anymore."

The township of Biruji was, as promised, larger than Mathis. The main road ran through the center of the town. Wooden buildings and temporary tents lined the street on either side. Painted signs hung from overhangs or swung on chains on large wooden arms over the street.

General Merchandise

Bazaar

Barber

Rooms to Let

Music and lights flooded the area from a two-story building on the corner. Built from a mix of stone, mortar, and wood, it was the most permanent building there. It was painted red and white with ornate shutters. Its windows were adorned with colorful lace drapery.

"Abuelita's" the sign read.

Men and women gathered on the wooden porch around its double doors. They gave the group a wary eye as they walked past.

"Don't mind them." Kay Stone advised. She tipped her hat toward the group. Heads nodded in cautious acknowledgment. "Everyone is a little on edge right now. Granny has been doing her best to keep everyone in good spirits, but it only goes so far."

"Do you have a current headcount?" Jalin asked as they walked down the street. His dark eyes surveyed the townspeople as they passed. Eyes that had been judging the group were quickly cast aside once they realized who and what Jalin was.

"We just barely got an accurate census a week. People come and go from towns like this all the time. Shutting down the road was our only hope of containing anything."

"It was a wise move." Jalin agreed. He glanced over his shoulder briefly to make certain Esperanza and Lyric were keeping pace with them, then continued watching the area as they walked.

"The news... good and bad both... is that there are less than a dozen people unaccounted for."

"A dozen people, Peacekeeper? That's twelve too many. Many of them could be carriers." Esperanza interjected.

Kay nodded in response. "It appears to only be transmissible by bite, thankfully. If it were anything else, I think we would all be dead by now," Stone said as she lead the three into a large building.

She motioned to the room. "The Guild used this for storage and maintenance. The last four infected are in here. Normally, I would toss them in a cell, but they were still building the jail. I couldn't chance taking them to Tayler much less Mathis, to hold them, so we had to improvise."

The windows in the room were boarded up, and the large back doors appeared to be sealed. The gigantic room was devoid of its normal wares. The only items in place were a few tables, some chairs, and a wall of metal cages. The cages appeared to have been hastily constructed from various metal crates and cargo transports.

"They mine copper primarily up here, but someone is always hoping for silver or gold. Had to fill in an entire claim earlier in the season because the copper was full of hot metal. The whole team had to be sent down the mountain for healing. Poor bastards."

"And you are positive that is not what these are suffering from?" Esperanza asked quietly. She peered into the darkness toward the caged patients. Each cage held a cot and a bucket. The occupants of each cage were curled up in the far corners of their habitat. The cages themselves showed heavy signs of wear - the grating was stretched in a few places as if someone was trying to punch or rend their way out.

"Fever, nausea, fatigue... the symptoms were similar... at first. But hot-metal poison doesn't spread like this does."

"Who are they?" Lyric asked.

"Those two are locals here - Eddie and Javi. The woman there is Lisbeth, she's from Tayler. My best guess is she was visiting someone here when it happened. The last cage is Tomas... my cousin," she said. "They have been our 'guests' for the past week."

"I'm sorry," was all Lyric could offer.

Stone chewed on the inside of her cheek a moment. "Yeah, well... the sentiment is appreciated." She turned to the Inquisitors. "I guess it's your turn to figure this mess out. I need you to know I will not be opening those cages. I cannot take the chance of this spreading. Please understand that."

Esperanza nodded her head, "Understood completely, Sheriff. I will see what Hil can tell us."

"Oh, and... avoid getting bit. Inquisitors or not, I do have extra cages, and I will put you in them."

Jalin scoffed at the comment.

"And," Stone continued, "Don't step past that white chalk line. It marks the extent of their reach. They still grab when they get riled up. For now, they're quiet. But when the sun goes down, they get really... vocal."

Stone took a step away from the cages and toward the doors. "Ernie and Chuy will be at the doors here. When you're ready to come out, just knock. I have to oversee the morning census. I'll check back in an hour. Good luck."

Stone walked out and they could hear the doors being bolted.

Jalin looked at Lyric and nodded toward the back of the room and the walls. "They have gas lamps installed. See if you can turn them on to give us something to work with."

"Understood," Lyric said and walked toward the main doors, away from the cages. She followed the supply lines along the ceiling with her eyes. Cans of solvent and oil were stacked along the walls leading toward the office.

Jalin stretched and nodded to Esperanza. "When you are ready."

"Hil grant us clarity." She whispered as she wrapped her hand around the holy symbol of their shared faith.

Jalin narrowed his gaze and focused on the one called Javi. He stretched the fingers of his right hand in anticipation.

The occupants sat still and motionless in their respective prisons. Each huddled against the far wall, their faces turned away from all activity. As Esperanza's invocation filled the air, they twitched.

Lyric quickly made her way to a set of toggles just inside the door of the small office. With a pull upwards of one, there was a slight hiss as gas flowed through the lines. Pulling up the second, a series of clicks echoed overhead. Soft light gently pushed the shadows away.

Esperanza's eyes opened. The golden hue of Hill's illuminating vision filled her. She turned her focus on the four people in the cages across from her.

And screamed.

Chaos erupted from the cages. Inhuman wailing pierced the air as the occupants leaped up from their crouched positions and threw themselves against the bars of their makeshift prisons. Gutteral howls and hisses accompanied their wails. Jalin's trained reflexes responded instinctively, and with a quick flex of his arm, his blade extended and locked into place. Its long edge extending over the marked chalk line on the floor.

Javi hissed loudly and his hand darted out from between the bars. Long fingers wrapped around the blade, intent on grasping hold and pulling Jalin in. Jalin braced, ready for the pull. Ready for the slice of flesh along the sharpened edge. Instead, Javi howled in pain, as his hand began to smolder and sizzle. He yanked his hand away from the blessed silvered weapon and bared his teeth at the Inquisitor.

No. Not teeth. Rows of pointed fangs filled Javi's mouth.

As the lights came up fully, Jalin finally saw what they were facing. Pale-skinned, almost anemic faces with black-on-black eyes stared back at all of them. They hissed and howled from behind the bars of their cages, trying to find refuge from the light.

Jalin backed away from the creatures, holding his scoring blade between them for protection. His other hand reached for Esperanza.

"Back. Get back. Get away from them," he whispered urgently.

Lyric rushed forward and quickly placed her hand over Esperanza's eyes, breaking the vision's trance. The Voca collapsed into Lyric's arms.

Lyric's eyes darted toward the creatures and back to Jalin.

"What's wrong with them? What are they?"

Jalin turned fear-filled eyes toward the Imperial Scribe.

"Vampyres. They are all vampyres."

A Lifted Veil

"**B**ullshit!" Stone said as she slammed her hand on the table. "Those are nothing more than ghost stories designed to scare children into behaving."

"And I am certain no one gave weight to the thought of an army of ghouls before the Corpse Wars proved them all wrong," Jalin replied.

"It was three hundred years ago!"

"And how many ghouls have you killed in these hills in the last month, Peacekeeper?"

"Ghouls are not Vampyres, Inquisitor!" Stone insisted.

"Don't you think I know that?" Jalin countered.

"Vampyres were eradicated when the Primeras returned to the Place Beyond. We all know that!" Stone objected.

"Just because they haven't been seen doesn't mean they aren't still here," Jalin argued. He held up a warning hand to the Peacekeeper. "Believe what you will, Peacekeeper, but when I say that those creatures are not people anymore, perhaps you should listen to the person who has dedicated their life to their eradication."

The debate continued.

Lyric watched from across the room as both Inquisitors tried to explain the situation to Peacekeeper Stone to no avail. When Stone returned after the census, she found the storeroom locked with the three of them sitting around one table outside the doors. It started with a statement, which became an accusation, which evolved into an argument and eventually just became a shouting match.

She understood the hesitation and denial by Peacekeeper Stone. Even where Ladies in White and Werewolves were proven to walk the land, Vampyres were the stuff of legend. They were a story told to teach humility and to remind humanity of the failings of greed.

Long before the Death Mages came into existence, humankind first sought immortality. Legend spoke that Vampyres were created when humans stole the blood of the Primeras, the first people. But rather than making humans immortal creatures of unearthly beauty, what resulted was twisted and perverse. Hil then blessed humanity with the knowledge and skill to purge the world of these abominations. In punishment, the Primeras were forced to depart. They were the first children of the Heavens, and this world should have been theirs to protect. Instead, because of humanity's treachery and to stop more of these atrocities from being created, the Primeras begrudgingly accepted Hil's demands and went back to the Place Beyond. When they left, they took all their wisdom and teachings with them, leaving humanity to find their place in mortality alone.

No one remembered the entire story any longer, and there were no records left to verify how much of the oral tradition was accurate… or how much had become mere legend and myth. It was said that Hil's people purged the University Libraries of the records when they removed the tales of Hanwi from the books and scrolls there. Lyric never understood that. Removing written content did not remove it from cultural knowledge. The absence of a thing only made people want to learn more about it and recover what was lost.

The voices of the Peacekeeper and Inquisitors continued to rise, pulling Lyric from her internal musing. One guard standing across from the group shifted his weight from side to side. His fingers jerked and inched toward the butt of his pistol.

Jalin and Stone stood opposite each other, leaning over the table, nose to nose. Esperanza sat at Jalin's side, her focus on one deputy. Her long fingers almost imperceptibly traced a sigil on the surface of the table.

This is about to get ugly, Lyric thought.

Her eyes scoured around the room, hoping to find something she could use to distract them all and break the tension. Nothing was within reach.

She jabbed her hand into her satchel, retrieving her only true weapon.

A pot of scrivener's ink.

She thudded the glass ink pot down, catching the attention of those seated there. It tipped onto its side and rolled into the middle of the table. Multiple sets of eyes broke from each other and fell on the intruding glass jar.

Jalin's focus followed the ink pot's trajectory back to its origin point, his eyes locking on Lyric's.

She offered an uncomfortable smile.

"Apologies." She reached across the table to recover the offending item. The action had been enough. Jalin and Stone pulled away from one another. Esperanza folded her hands in her lap. The guard across the way settled back into an easy stance.

"If I may... ask a question or two?" Lyric asked. She pretended to fumble with the contents of her satchel and finally produced a small notebook. She glanced up at Jalin. He glowered at her, then rolled his eyes and motioned his hand dismissively at her.

"Proceed, Scribe Wax."

"Thank you, Inquisitor." She sniffed and nodded. "For the sake of posterity," she scribbled down a few notes on the paper. "We all agree that ghouls are creatures created when spirits...usually mad or malevolent spirits ... attempt to inhabit a corpse. Yes?" Lyric asked as she scribbled away.

Lyric's words gave both groups a moment's pause and forced them to consider. The vein on Jalin's forehead throbbed and Esperanza's expression was chill, but both nodded in agreement. Stone, whose face was flushed, hesitantly accepted the definition as well.

"Thank you." She nodded and continued to write. "Regarding the individuals in the cages in the other room. Inquisitor Cortez, for the record, can you please state the physical differences you observed in these persons versus what one would typically see in ghouls?" The Scribe asked.

Jalin took a deep breath and nodded. "The skin of the afflicted differs from a ghoul."

"In what way?" Lyric asked.

"Lack of decay."

"Explain?"

"The body of a ghoul is deceased, and though animated, it does not cease to decay. There is no decay on these creatures and no scent of graverot."

"Is that important?"

"Graverot is a chief characteristic associated with ghoul infestation. These creatures are not rotting. They appear desiccated, lacking internal moisture. Their skin is pale and stretched tightly over their sinews."

"Thank you, Inquisitor." Lyric glanced at Stone. The Peacekeeper was standing with their arms folded across her chest as she listened to the information. "What else?" Lyric asked Jalin.

Cortez considered for a moment. "The afflicted are strong and remarkably quick. If you examine the bars on the cages, you note that some of them have been bent." He looked at Stone. "They will not hold indefinitely. Ghouls possess neither strength nor speed."

"I see," Lyric commented. "Are there other physical differences?"

Jalin nodded. "Ghouls are spirits trapped in a dead body. They do not possess the ability to change that body, or cause it to react as it did when it was living." Jalin looked across the table at Stone. "The eyes on the creatures still dilate when exposed to a light source... and they have extra teeth."

"What?" Stone asked.

"Additional sets of teeth. Like an eel. Ghouls cannot force a body to grow an additional set of razor-sharp teeth in its mouth."

Stone narrowed her eyes. "That doesn't mean they are Vampyres. They could be something else. Something we haven't seen."

Jalin held up a hand in pause. "I will grant you it is possible that a Death Mage is experimenting with creating some new horror to unleash upon the world. It would be well within their design to do so." He gestured to Esperanza. "But I shall defer to the Voca on this last piece."

Stone glanced over at Esperanza. There was hesitation in the Peacekeeper's eyes.

"I have a deep respect for the blessings of Hil, Inquisitor Boyorquez... however."

Esperanza stood from her chair and slowly smoothed back her hair. The brilliant saffron yellow of her tunic was faded with road dirt, and there were dark hollows beginning to form beneath her eyes. Despite this, there was still an air of almost regal dignity to her.

"Touching the brilliance of Hil can be a humbling experience, Peacekeeper. I can understand your hesitation."

She tugged on the cuffs of her sleeves. "What is one of Hil's chief tenants?"

The Peacekeeper frowned and considered Esperanza's words. She stumbled over her response, "Erm, truth?" she stammered.

Esperanza smiled warmly in response. "Indeed. To bring the light of truth to the shadows of darkness and deceit. I am, therefore, incapable of showing you anything that is not true under the Light of Hil's vision."

Stone considered Esperanza's words. She reached up and rubbed her face with her weathered hands.

"Fine. Fine. I consent."

Esperanza nodded and stepped around the edge of the table. "I will grant you the ability to see what I can see... for a moment. It is a simple blessing."

Stone sucked on her tooth and nodded.

"Inquisitor Boyorquez?" Lyric interrupted.

Esperanza turned to look at the Scribe. "Ms. Wax?"

"I believe it would aid in confirming this claim if I could bear witness as well?"

"No! Absolutely not!" Jalin interjected.

Lyric flinched slightly at the harshness of Jalin's tone. Her reaction was clearly not lost on him.

"It's far too dangerous," he added.

Esperanza pursed her lips and looked between the Scribe and her partner. "Should it not be her decision?"

Jalin turned hard eyes on Esperanza. "She's a child. She doesn't understand."

"It is her Verdad, Cortez. Her quest for truth. Hil has led her here. Do you doubt Hil's wisdom and protection?"

"Never." the word was cold.

"Then have faith and believe that she has been chosen for this."

Jalin's eyes lifted to meet Lyric's as she stood at the other end of the table from them. She smiled softly in reply and nodded.

"I cannot live in obscurity, Inquisitor Cortez. Not if I am to take up the pen and be a recorder of history." She stepped around the table and walked to him. Looking up, she studied his rich maple-colored eyes, and the scars on his face. The lessons of his life, were etched and carved into his flesh for the world to see.

"You discharge your duty to me with honor. Thank you for your protection."

Jalin blinked. A moment of confusion danced behind his stoney eyes at her words. He nodded uncomfortably and stepped back slightly. "Of course." he cleared his throat and looked to Esperanza. "Voca."

Esperanza nodded, "Very well. What you will see will last for but a moment, but I can end the vision if what you see is too much." She looked between both Stone and Lyric. "There is no shame in flinching. We are mortal beings, after all. I will stand between the two of you. You will face the door with your eyes closed. Inquisitor Cortez will open the door. I will touch your forehead with my fingertips. You will feel a sensation of warmth. When I tell you, open your eyes, and all will be revealed."

Both women did as instructed. Stone settled into place with a stalwart countenance on her tired face. Lyric glanced briefly at Jalin and then at Esperanza. The Voca stared back at Lyric, an unspoken question in her own eyes. Lyric nodded then and closed her eyes.

The touch on her forehead was gentle, like the lips of a mother on a sleeping child, careful not to wake them from their sleep. Warmth blossomed on her skin, surrounding her. It was comforting and almost familiar. A hug from a loved one, but more.

She heard Esperanza's voice, instructing her to open her eyes and to look at the deputies first slowly. Lyric slowly opened her eyes and saw the two men standing there who had been there a moment earlier. There was a light that emanated from them now, that was visible to her. The pulse of life, as well as the gray weight of fear weighing down upon them.

Lyric turned her gaze to Jalin. His face was the same hardened face she had stared at moments earlier, but the light of life burned around him. There was no grey weight of fear present on him. Instead, a reddish hue pulsed deep within his chest. Passion? Rage? She could not tell. She continued to stare at the red light, curiosity nagging at her mind.

Peacekeeper Stone screamed and fell to the ground. The trance of the divine sight broken.

"Take it off! Take it off!" Stone begged.

Esperanza rushed over to the Peacekeeper and waved her hand over her forehead. "Breath, just breath - it will pass."

Lyric blinked and shook her head. The Sight was still upon her, though the almost hypnotic trance was gone. She looked at Jalin. His expression was dark as he watched the Peacekeeper on the floor. He looked at Lyric.

"Be careful and know when to look away," he cautioned.

She nodded her head carefully and turned to face the cages.

It was dark, but the darkness was not empty. The space around the cages changed and warped, like the ripples on a pond of water. Power. It rippled off of each creature; the waves getting smaller farther away until they merged with the darkness. In the center of each person was an inky mass, undulating and roiling. It curled and coiled like a nest of snakes. She stared into the inky darkness, watching the swells and waves, feeling a pull tugging on her gently. A chill washed across her skin. Empty black eyes turned to look at her from across the room. Another pull. A feeling of want. Of need. Dark eyes became rimmed in red. The undulating mass of gloom roiled faster. Ripples pushing farther out. Reaching.

Hunger.

Tendrils of darkness oozed toward her, seeking to envelop her and pull her in. Tiny snake-like coils with maws of razor-sharp teeth like shards of glass stretched toward her.

Light.

A blinding, exhilarating light washed over her and engulfed her, banishing the darkness. As it retreated, she heard a noise, like a rabbit screaming in a snare. Then she was surrounded in warmth and filled with joy and adoration. Its beauty was without comparison and beyond description.

Hil. This was the love of Hil. And there were no words.

Lyric felt her chest tighten and wetness on her face, and then warm hands on her cheeks. A voice speaking to her, calling to her. But it was distant and muffled.

Lyric. Come home.

And it was gone.

She found herself collapsed on the floor of the office, wrapped in the arms of Inquisitor Boyorquez. Her throat felt raw, as if she had been crying or screaming. Her legs were weak, and her body ached.

"What... what happened?" Lyric asked.

Esperanza pulled back and looked into Lyric's face. Her thumbs gently wiped around her eyes and across her cheeks. She leaned forward and placed her lips on the young woman's forehead. "You are safe now." She whispered.

Lyric stared at Esperanza. Confusion in her eyes. She looked away from the woman, seeking Jalin's figure. He was standing between them and the warehouse door, scoring blade extended at the ready.

"They called to you." He retracted his blade. "And you listened. Boyorquez stopped you," Jalin said.

She looked at the others, and all gave a nod of agreement. Lyric looked down at her hands, and then back to Esperanza, "What was I looking at?"

Esperanza met Lyric's questioning gaze. "Corruption, dear child. Ancient, and original." She unfolded herself from her place on the floor and stood. Then offered her hand to Lyric.

"That is the difference. If those were ghouls, you would have seen the spirit that was riding the corpse. That? That is something very different."

"What is it?" Lyric stood.

"Man's first sin of hubris embodied," Jalin replied cooly, joining his partner and the scribe. "And a desire to spread."

Lyric blanched, and her knees buckled slightly. Jalin snapped out his hand, but she caught herself on the edge of the table and steadied her stance. "Thank you, Inquisitor. I will be fine."

"Your bravery is commendable, but you should sit," Esperanza instructed and guided Lyric back to her chair.

Lyric sat and took a deep breath.

Jalin set a large cup down in front of her. It smelled deeply of dark beer. He nodded at the cup. "It helps."

"Undoubtedly," Lyric replied. She drank from the cup, then set it down and reached for her pen once more. She cleared her throat. "Peacekeeper Stone - based on the experience, knowledge and evidence, do you now agree with the Inquisitor's assessment?"

Stone sat quietly at the other end of the table, tears on her face. She nodded, "Yes I do. My apologies to you both. What will Hil have us do?"

Jalin looked at the scoring blade on his arm and then back to Stone. "We need to lay them to rest."

Fire kills most things. That's what Hil taught us.

The words of Dr. Miracle in Mathis echoed in Lyric's mind. How does one kill something that has not been recorded as existing in over a millennium? Could it even be killed?

She stood by the open doorway and watched as the deputy, his name was Chuy, picked up a bucket of linseed oil and walked toward the cages. Several local carpenters had stored their finishing products in the warehouse. Among them was a barrel of oil. What would have been used to bring beauty to a masterpiece now would end a menace.

"Chuy, it doesn't have to be you," Stone interjected.

The burly deputy simply shook his head as he stepped up to the cage that held Javi. Tears stained Chuy's face as he stared at the creature that was once been his husband.

"He's the only thing I cared about in this world," Chuy replied. The creature opposite him stared blankly back. Its lips pulled back into a tooth-filled snarl. Chuy set his jaw. "You don't deserve to wear his skin!" He grabbed the bottom edge of the bucket and hurled the contents onto the creature. It wailed and howled and hissed in response.

"No!" Lyric gasped. She moved to step forward. Jalin's iron grasp wrapped around her arm and held her in place. She whipped her head around to glare at him. He simply shook his head in response and then released her.

"It has to be done."

Chuy reached into his pocket and pulled out a box of wooden matches. Stepping away from the fumes, he struck a match and tossed it forward. "Goodbye."

The match flew forward, igniting the volatile substance almost instantly. The fire raced and engulfed the creature in a wreath of whitish-yellow flames. An inhuman scream erupted from it as it surged toward the bars and slammed into them. The other three creatures joined the howls and echoed the same ear-piercing death wail. The sound was deafening.

Chuy and Stone clasped their hands over their ears and collapsed on the ground, writhing in pain. The windows cracked.

Lyric's head felt like it was on fire. The sound from the creatures burned in her ears and on her skin. Her vision swam.

"Jalin!" she called and grabbed at the Inquisitor, who wrapped his hands around her to hold her up.

"Boyorquez!" he shouted.

Nodding her head, the Voca forced herself to stand and walk toward the creatures. Stone and Chuy writhed on the floor, holding their hands over their ears. The windows continued to crack. One by one, they shattered. Broken glass raining down inside the warehouse.

A shockwave of pain slammed into Esperanza. She wrapped her hand around Hil's sigil and called on the God's protection. Raising her arms above her head, power coalesced into a large sphere of golden-reddish light. It surrounded her like a golden shield.

"Hil who brings light to the world," The Voca intoned, summoning the power of her God into her body, "Cleanse these bodies of their corruption. *Voluntad de Dios*!"

With a single motion, she threw her arms wide and four beams of energy surged out from the sphere, striking each creature. Engulfed by the light and held in place, the inhuman howling ceased. Their bodies slowly darkened like burning wood, cracks of light spreading over them, then they crumbled into chunks of ashy embers and dust.

The sphere faded from view, and Esperanza collapsed into unconsciousness.

THE COMING STORM

Peacekeeper Stone's assessment of how many people were missing or unaccounted for was wrong.

The moment Chuy set alight the fire in the warehouse, unearthly sounds erupted from the mountains surrounding the village of Biruji. It was a deep guttural noise, followed by clicks and moaning. Lyric had heard the howls of wolves in the past. This was not wolves.

The sounds seemed to bounce from location to location in the hills above Biruji. One group would end and another would begin seamlessly. It was difficult to determine how many sources of sound there were from the constant noise. The local villagers retreated indoors, barring and locking their doors and windows against whatever enemy threatened their homes. Some brave few gathered their belongings and attempted to leave for Mathis. They were stopped by Stone's deputies and forced to turn back.

Sunset would come soon, and the minions of the undead would find strength in Hil's absence from the skies overhead. Until the situation was contained, no one would be leaving.

Lyric sat next to the bed Esperanza slept in. Jalin had collected the fallen body of his partner after her collapse in the warehouse. Her magic had accomplished what it was called for. The four afflicted persons had been purged of their corruption and their bodies destroyed. Only ash remained. Now she lay unconscious in a bedroom at Abuelita's while Jalin and Stone prepared the village for whatever was coming next.

The Voca stirred slightly. Lyric reached out to take her hand. Esperanza's eyes fluttered as she forced herself into consciousness. Her head lolled to the side. She wet her dry lips with her tongue. "How long?" she whispered.

"Three hours," Lyric replied. She squeezed Esperanza's hand and released it, then reached for a water pitcher and glass.

Esperanza shifted and slowly forced herself into a seated position. She glanced around the room, trying to focus her eyes. "Where?"

"Abuelita's. Cortez said it was the most defensible location in the village, and he was uncertain how long you would be out." She poured a glass of water and offered it to Esperanza. The Voca nodded her head in thanks and sipped from the glass. Then she frowned.

"Those sounds..."

"They haven't stopped since... since the warehouse." Lyric offered, "They seem to increase. Two or three will wail or click or moan, then it fades, and another group takes over from a different direction. He can't pinpoint them."

Esperanza's brow furrowed. "But... I destroyed them..."

Lyric looked down at her hands and then back up at the woman laying in the bed. "The ones in the cells, yes."

The color drained from Esperanza's exhausted face. "How many?"

Lyric shook her head. "He doesn't know. Cortez thinks the wailing in the warehouse... when the fire started... wasn't a scream of pain, but a call to arms. A call for help."

"But that would mean... "

"There are enough worth calling? They are organized? They care about their fellows? They are being led?" Lyric said softly. She nodded and poured herself a glass of water as well. "Yes. A conversation I had with him before he left to secure the area. One he was not happy to entertain." She drank from her glass. "He believes more are coming and, based on Stone's accounts, they will attack when the sun sets, " Lyric said. "He hasn't said it, but I think Cortez is hoping you will be ready when they arrive."

"Hypocrisy, thy name is Jalin Cortez..." Esperanza said, then looked up at Lyric. "Apologies, Ms. Wax."

"Lyric." She corrected gently. "I think we've been through enough together to forgo the formalities if that is ok with you?"

Esperanza searched Lyric's face for a moment and then nodded somberly. "It is." She shifted in the bed and moved her legs to the edge. She closed her eyes and took a deep breath, steadying herself. "How much do you know about theurgy or the lesser sorceries? "

Lyric set her glass aside and turned to face Esperanza, giving the Voca her full attention. "Very little, honestly. I sat in on an introductory class one spring, but not being a practitioner, it was all theory... clearly."

Esperanza nodded. "All magic, even the Gifts of the Divine, can be dangerous. Not only to those around us but to the practitioner as well. Those who reach too far, or too fast..." she paused a moment, clearly considering her words, "The mortal body was not designed to channel the Gifts of the Divine. Insanity. Mutation. Death. These can be the cost of wielding such power. Hil chose me to carry a sliver of a spark of their Divinity. Chosen or not, my frame is still mortal. Still human."

"It could kill you?" Lyric asked.

"Voca have died in service of Hil, yes." Esperanza reached out and took Lyric's hands into hers. "Jalin knows that when the time comes, I will do everything I can to protect the innocent. No matter the cost to myself."

"Esperanza..."

The Voca shook her head. "This is what I have been called to, and what I have promised. Jalin Cortez... for good or ill... is my Manos. My Hand. He will ensure that... should I fall... the enemy will not recover my body."

A chill ran down Lyric's spine at her words. She shook her head and tried to pull away. Esperanza's grip tightened slightly.

"Lyric, you need to hear this."

"No!"

"Scribe Wax, hear my truth!" the Voca said. She continued. "If I fall, there is no telling what horror I will become if they are permitted to gain access to my body. It. Cannot. Happen."

Tears welled in Lyric's eyes as she listened to the woman across from her.

"Jalin understands what needs to be done. I need you too, as well. Please."

"Voca…"

"If I have fallen, and we are to be overwhelmed," the Inquisitor reached into her robe and withdrew a small silver vial. "I cannot allow Hil's power to fall into their hands. If I fall, simply open this and pour it on me. That is all. Nothing more."

Concerned, Lyric eyed the small container. "What is it?"

"'Hil's Blood." Esperanza replied. "It will ignite with the air and a golden flame will consume anything in the area in a matter of seconds." She tucked it away into a pocket of her robe. "I keep it here… should you need it," She looked back into Lyric's face and met her sad eyes. "You have been a worthy companion, Lyric Wax. Should the time come, I know you would be welcomed at Hil's side," Esperanza said quietly.

"I… I understand," Lyric said after a moment. The weight of the unspoken offer felt heavy and left her uneasy.

"Two more things, Lyric. Let Cortez know I will be ready when the time comes," she asked.

Nodding her head, Lyric stood. "And the second?"

"Anza - for moments like these and maybe in the future, just call me Anza," the Inquisitor said as she laid back down on the bed.

Lyric found Jalin on the edge of town, staring into the darkness of a mineshaft. She had inquired after the irritable Inquisitor after leaving Esperanza to rest. Despite Cortez's distrust of magic, her link to the Divine would be needed in the upcoming battle.

The village was bustling with activity. Doors were being sealed and windows boarded up. Residents were moved from the far ends of the township and placed in shared buildings that were more defensible. Those not able to fight were secured in the basement of Abuelita's. Lacking a Shrine, the stonework building was the strongest in the village. A pair of guards were assigned the duty of defending the building and its inhabitants. Those consigned to the basement were quickly put to work sharpening pick axes and shovels - the only edged weapons available. Stone inventoried a dozen sledgehammers. These were handed out to be used in defense of the town and each other as well. Torches, lanterns, and rags soaked in lamp oil and stuffed into bottles. These were the weapons of people who understood the dangers of dwelling beyond the protection of Imperial Walls.

Lyric watched as they all worked together, grimly determined to make the best of a dire situation. They understood that a good deal of them may not survive the night, but none questioned what was being asked of them. This was the world the Corpse Wars left behind.

The unearthly sounds from the creatures continued, echoing off of the mountainside and down the valleys. How many they were, or where they would come from when they chose to attack, no one knew. Each building had to be prepared to defend itself and its occupants. And to stand without expectation of aid from anyone else, as there was no one else to call upon.

Fire kills most things.

It was the mantra they held onto as they filled bottles with linseed oil and handed them out. Two to every building being defended. If the creatures broke in, and it looked like they were going to lose, set the bottles on fire, throw them at the enemy, and pray for Hil's guiding light.

Stone was not keen to embrace the finality of the situation until she was reminded of the warehouse and what happened there. Ultimately, the Peacekeeper accepted what needed to be done and set herself to the task. She handed out rifles and pistols and what ammunition there was. Those with practiced aim were placed in attics. Bullets would slow the creatures, but would not kill them. Enough shots to the head should stop anything, though. Or that was the hope.

Lyric approached Jalin carefully, mindful of his edginess and the scoring blade on his forearm. She cleared her throat.

Jalin dipped his head in her direction without turning to face her. "Ms. Wax."

"The last of the tools have been delivered. Stone is doing one last check on them all," Lyric said.

Jalin nodded, continuing to stare into the dark maw of the mountainside. Lyric's eyes followed his and stared into the darkness, looking for any sign of movement. Nothing stirred.

"A fallback position?" She asked quietly.

Jalin shook his head. "No. It would be suicide to hold up in there. If we had more time... and resources... we might lure them into the mine and seal it, however..."

"There would be no way to know they were destroyed?"

"Precisely."

The Scribe stepped up to stand next to the Inquisitor. She chewed on her bottom lip for a moment and shoved her hands into her pockets, uncertain how to proceed.

"They're a myth, you know?" Jalin commented. "Vampyres. The true boogeymen of the undead world," he whispered.

Lyric said nothing, but nodded her head and listened.

"The stuff of nightmares," Jalin said. His voice was flavored with a hint of awe. "Manos are required to study and understand all the creatures of the world, both natural and unnatural. We are trained on how to deal with them. To hunt them. To end them. But this... " he motioned to the darkness, " this is not something any Inquisitor has ever dealt with. These creatures were nothing more than stories ages before the Order was ever formed. How does mortal man destroy a legend?"

Lyric regarded Cortez for a moment. Was his awe inspired by fear... or admiration? Her gaze drifted to him and lingered for a moment as she considered his words.

"Was not mortal man responsible for their creation?" she asked.

Jalin pursed his lips. "That is one story, yes."

"There are others?" Lyric asked.

Jalin shrugged slightly. "How many versions of the same myth wander these lands, Ms. Wax?" He turned slightly to face her. "As a Scribe, surely you understand the answer to your own question."

"A fair reply. Forgive me."

A howl in the distance drew Jalin's attention. He tilted his head to the side and closed his eyes to listen. The fingers on his right hand danced lightly along the handle of a hunting knife tucked into his belt.

"The dream and dread of every Manos... " he breathed, listening.

Lyric frowned. Cortez's tone was filled with what could only be described as longing. An aching desire that was almost painful to hear. She pulled her left hand out of her pocket and paused, just shy of reaching for him.

"To die in the embrace of the unknown?" Lyric asked.

Jalin's eyes opened, and he turned to look at Lyric. "To end ancient evil," he replied. He stared deeply into Lyric's grey-green eyes, his gaze both piercing and unsettling. She shivered. He raised a rough and calloused hand and paused a moment before he lay it gently on the side of her pale face. "To preserve innocence. No matter the cost."

Lyric swallowed deeply as she stood before the Hand of Hil. The Hunter. The Inquisitor. His eyes, the color of rich amber syrup, stared into the depths of her soul with an insight honed by hunting the unnatural.

A growling moan sounded from somewhere above them. Jalin's eyes snapped away from Lyric and sought to focus on the source. His lithe body was at once taught and ready to spring into action. His scoring blade was brought to the fore, his other arm held out in a protective gesture.

"Where are you?" he whispered, almost eagerly.

Concern welled up in Lyric's chest. She had seen the devout protector in Jalin before. The errant detective, the responsible soldier, and the dutiful son, but this was something else. This was the Hunter. In that moment of concern, she finally understood what disturbed Esperanza Boyorques about her partner.

They had raised him to be a killer. To hunt the hunters of the night. To give no quarter when faced with the evil that lurked in the darkness. No matter the face it wore. No matter the name it took. As Jalin's eyes searched the hillside, Lyric wondered how many people had ever seen this side of the man and lived.

To preserve innocence, no matter the cost.

Lyric reached up and placed her fingertips over her skin where he had touched her. Her breath caught in her throat. She quickly covered her mouth with her hand and swallowed down her desire to weep for the loss of a soul. She wanted to scream, to swear, to rail at the Inquisition for fashioning a program that would do this to someone. She wanted to draw him away from his search, change the subject, turn this version of the man off, and lock it away.

It was at that moment her prayers were unfortunately answered.

"It's stopped," Cortez said

Lyric dropped her hand and looked around. Pushing away her previous thoughts, she focused and instead listened.

The howls and wailing had ceased. In their place now was nothing but a heavy silence.

"Something happened. We need to prepare," Jalin said and quickly spun heel back toward the town.

Lyric stared into the darkness of the mine shaft a moment longer before turning and following. She had seen the darkness and red rage within the man. Quietly, she hoped that rage would never see her.

SCREAMS OF BATTLE

The atmosphere crackled with tension as haunting howls reverberated across the rugged terrain. A feeling in the air shifted as it grew heavy with an eerie silence and people anxiously surveyed the horizon. The once palpable tension gradually morphed into a pernicious blend of paranoia and fear. Lyric trailed behind the Inquisitor as they returned to the town's heart, only to find the Peacekeeper encircled by a fervent crowd.

"We don't know what the hell they are doing, but I would *not* take it as a sign that they left!" Stone said firmly to one man. "Now get back to your posts. It will be dark soon, and we all have to be prepared."

While the lingering paranoia still gripped their minds, the group slowly dispersed as Stone strode toward Lyric and her companion.

"I've fortified the road with a stronger barrier," she announced. "If things escalate beyond control, the guards will ignite it and retreat to Abeulita's. It's the most defensible location in the vicinity. If a final stand becomes necessary, that's where it will occur. And if we survive to see another day, at least we won't starve."

Lyric glanced at Jalin and noticed him absentmindedly chewing on the inside of his cheek, his gaze scanning the landscape. It was evident that he was only partially attentive to Stone's words, his eyes widening and narrowing as he scrutinized the sky. He was grappling with something and deep in thought. Following his line of sight, she sought to decipher the source. As she looked up, the sky's vermillion hue signaled the sun's imminent descent below the horizon.

"Problem?" asked Stone.

With a nod of his head, Jalin spoke, though it was evident that his words were not directed at Lyric and Stone. "The initial howl... it wasn't just a call for help," he explained. "Wild dogs, and even wolves, communicate like that, but it's usually brief. These creatures, however, kept howling intermittently, and the sounds never came from the same direction..." His eyes widened, and then he locked eyes with Stone. "Tell everyone to keep the lights up, start lighting those fires now!"

As Stone hurried away to relay the urgent instructions, Esperanza approached slowly. "What's happening?" she inquired.

"After that initial wail, the relentless calls continued without respite. It was a calculated tactic, meant to keep us in a state of fear and unease," Jalin explained to her.

"Wait, are you seriously suggesting that these creatures can plan?" Esperanza asked. Lyric could see the fear and realization creeping into Voca's chest. The beings in the cages appeared more like savage animals, but this revelation hinted at something far more sinister. The memory of the darkness emanating from them resurfaced and, once again, she envisioned those haunting, black eyes. How much of their gaze was filled with baleful intelligence?

"Hyenas exhaust their prey through relentless harassment before going in for the kill. These people have had little rest and were subjected to those howls all day while working. This... this was a deliberate strategy," Jalin muttered, shaking his head. "I hope you've rested as much as possible. Tonight, we cannot succumb to human weakness. Hil's light must not falter."

It was difficult to discern whether his last statement was intended as a cutting remark or an awkward attempt at a pep talk. Regardless, Esperanza's expression remained unchanged. The Voca stood resolute, her voice unwavering.

"Where do you need me to be?" she asked.

Just as Jalin was about to speak, the howls erupted once more, but this time they were different. Interwoven with the howls were hoots and hisses, indicating multiple people. Yet there was a distinct change in tone. It was as if they were goading each other, fueling their malevolence. Lyric turned to Jalin, expecting to find him focused on the source of the howls but his gaze was fixed on the darkness surrounding them. And then it hit them—the putrid stench of decaying flesh, unmistakable and ominous.

Graverot.

"Quickly, to Abuelita's!" Jalin urged. "If something comes at you, don't hesitate! Kill it before it kills you!"

As chaos engulfed the town, gunshots resonated, mingling with the sound of splintering wood and the cacophony of people's shouts. The guards at the gate acted swiftly, setting the barrier ablaze, while their comrades unleashed a barrage of bullets upon the encroaching shadowy figures. With a sense of urgency, the men and women of the mining encampment sprinted into various buildings, their battle cries piercing the air as they swung pickaxes to fend off the undead abominations. The outcome hung precariously in the balance, the fine line between success and failure, life and death becoming ever more tenuous.

Lyric and Esperanza dashed towards the towering structure ahead. From its windows, long guns protruded, firing shots at unseen targets. Casting a quick glance behind her, Lyric spotted Jalin, surveying their surroundings while preparing himself for the impending onslaught.

The front porch of Abeulita's was fortified with an improvised barricade comprising minecarts, metal rails, and chicken wire. The door to the building was tightly shut, but Stone waved them in. Just a few more yards, Lyric thought, and she could seize a rifle and join the battle, striving to stem the tide of darkness threatening to engulf them all.

A jarring impact sent Lyric sprawling to the ground, her breath forcibly expelled from her lungs. The phrase "having your bell rung" took on a whole new meaning as she grappled with disorientation. The collision and the subsequent strike of her head against the earth left her reeling. As she regained her bearings, the sickening sound of her cured leather armor cracking filled her ears. Monsterous hands clamped tightly around her shoulders, forcing her down. Opening her eyes, she found herself face to face with a woman, whose eyes were dark pools devoid of humanity glistened with an otherworldly gleam. The woman's gaping maw bared a menacing row of yellowed, sharpened teeth. Time stood still, and Lyric had no opportunity to react or think. She closed her eyes, bracing for the worst.

Suddenly, a piercing scream shattered the air, accompanied by the sounds of struggle. The creature relinquished its grip on Lyric's shoulders. Hastily reopening her eyes, she saw golden hands grappling with the creature and pulling it away from her. It was Esperanza, the Voca, radiating a fiery golden aura as she fought to free Lyric from the clutches of the abomination.

Smoke rose and flesh sizzled as Esperanza wrestled with the creature.

"Take its head!" the Inquisitor shouted, her voice resolute as she delivered a powerful kick to the back of the creature's legs and forced it to its knees.

Amidst the chaos of gunshots and screams, both human and unholy, Lyric understood her mission. Drawing her short blade from its sheath, she took a deep breath and swung at the creature's head. The strike did not sever the neck, but pierced the base of the skull. The creature howled and convulsed, yet Esperanza's grip remained firm. Pulling her blade back, Lyric observed fetid blood oozing up from the wound and leaking like a faulty pipe. Suppressing her revulsion, she prepared to strike again and locked eyes with the vampyre. It bellowed in furious rage, but Lyric refused to be daunted. Responding with a fierce scream of her own, she swung the blade with all her might and cleaved the creature's face and head.

The creature convulsed again, finally ceasing its movements as Esperanza released it. A burst of gunshots erupted behind Lyric, capturing her attention. She turned to witness Jalin locked in combat with another vampyre. His long coat was torn, but his movements were fluid and deadly, reminiscent of a skilled dancer. He displayed lethal agility, each elegant strike willed with unforgiving destruction. The creature hissed, as Jalin pummeled its face with an empty pistol. Despite being shot multiple times in the chest and having its foot severed at the ankle, it strove to stand. Jalin pressed forward, his blade descending with each fatal flourish. The vampyre attempted to retreat but the relentless onslaught continued. The blade slashed into its chest, causing sizzling flesh and agonized screams, forcing it to stumble backward.

Distracted by Jalin's display of lethal grace, Lyric was startled by a tug at her hip. Glancing over, she saw Esperanza had drawn her pistol and was firing at one of the nearby buildings. A vampyre had already ascended the small structure, tearing off a section of the roof. Despite the shots, the vampyre continued to ravage the roof, exposing the shooter inside. More gunshots erupted from the exposed crawl space, but the vampyre pounced, crashing through the roof and into the building.

In the distance, the cacophony of panicked screams and enraged roars blended with ghoulish howls of bloodlust. Two buildings were engulfed in flames, their occupants' fates uncertain. Slower figures lurched into the light. While illuminated by the fires, a group of miners fiercely wielded their pickaxes against the wave of new creatures. Ghouls—spawned by the vampyres—leaped onto the bodies of the injured and dying. Lyric positioned herself with her back against the barrier, scanning her surroundings. Between the alleyways, she noticed someone tending to a fallen body. An instinct to rush over and offer aid surged within her but she hesitated as the person turned towards her. Despite the shadows obscuring their appearance, there was something unsettling about their presence. Rising to their feet, they walked into the light and dragged the body along after them. Fresh blood covered their face and chest, their clothing in tatters. Locking eyes with Lyric, the vampyre let out a piercing scream. Abandoning the body, it charged towards her with unnatural speed. Lyric swiftly drew her second pistol and fired. Simultaneously, a thundering volley of shots erupted from the long guns within the mine cart barrier. The intense barrage pounded the creature, tearing a fist-sized hole in its chest and causing it to stagger. The vampyre stumbled toward Lyric, collapsing in a heap a few yards from her.

Emerging from behind her, Peacekeeper Stone marched past Lyric, relentlessly firing shot after shot into the creature's body as it labored to rise. With a swift motion, Stone swung the shotgun off her shoulder and thrust its dual barrels into the vampyre's howling maw before pulling the trigger. The creature's head erupted into a grotesque rain of gore, Stone's war cry piercing the pandemonium around them. Reloading her weapons, she barked orders to concentrate their fire on the approaching parties of ghouls. Turning back to Lyric, Stone shouted for the Scribe to fall behing the barrier, her pistol aimed at the advancing ghouls. Shot after shot rang out as Stone urged those who could hear to retreat to Abuelita's. Lyric reloaded her pistol, momentarily distracted by the Peacekeeper's fierce determination when suddenly the entire area was bathed in light.

Esperanza stood at the center of the battle her arms raised high as a radiant ball of light as brilliant as the morning sun illuminated the surroundings. As Lyric turned away from the blinding light, she witnessed Jalin's blade emerging from the back of another vampyre, causing the creature to convulse in pain and anger. Its flesh sizzled under the divine blaze. With his free hand, Jalin repeatedly stabbed the creature in the face, as he screamed fiercely. All around them, ghouls and vampyres shrieked in agony as the radiant light seared into their beings. Ghouls attempted to flee, only to be struck down by pickaxes and shovels.

In her peripheral vision, Lyric caught a blur of movement. Turning her gaze, she spotted a vampyre sprinting blindly toward Esperanza. The intense light scorched away its flesh, exposing the rotting muscles beneath, yet it did not deter the creature's frenzied pursuit of the Inquisitor. Lyric wanted to call out to Jalin but a quick glance revealed he was immersed in his own bloodlust, rushing headlong into the remaining pack of ghouls. Resigned to her only course of action, Lyric drew her blade and dashed forward to intercept the imminent threat. The creature leapt toward Esperanza but collided with Lyric instead. She drove her sword into the creature as they were propelled backward, crashing into the minecart barrier. Time slowed as Lyric and the screaming vampyre were sent hurtling through the air. Twisting the sword, Lyric unleashed a defiant yell as the blinding light consumed her vision. In an instant, there was a resounding clang of metal, searing pain, and then Lyric's world plunged into darkness.

Seated at an antique desk, she basked in the soft embrace of sunlight that poured through the open windows and cast a warm glow upon her surroundings. The weathered, leather-bound book with its pages adorned by a mesmerizing array of illustrations, lay open before her. Each page unfolded a tapestry of ethereal faces and enchanting creatures, their names obscured by a haze of mystery. In these depictions, a delicate balance between otherworldly beauty and spine-tingling horror danced, captivating her senses. Familiarity tugged at her consciousness, yet the threads connecting these images to her memories remained elusive. Was she traversing the halls of the revered Grand Archives, or had she stumbled upon an altogether different realm, shrouded in its own secrets? The question swirled in her mind, a riddle begging to be solved.

Aching for connection, she desperately longed to share her bewildering experiences. Her gaze wandered through the expanse surrounding her, hoping to find solace in the presence of another soul. Yet, the vastness of the room offered naught but solitude, broken only by towering shelves that housed countless tomes and meticulously preserved manuscripts. A labyrinth of wisdom and forgotten tales stretched into the distance, each shelf whispering untold stories, yearning for a fugitive audience in this moment of desolation.

Summoning her resolve, she rose from her seat, her eyes tracing the library's expanse. And there, like a fleeting mirage amidst an ocean of knowledge, she caught sight of movement to her left. Her gaze narrowed, fixating on the figure who stood gracefully before one of the lofty shelves. Silently, with a gentle touch, they returned a weathered tome to its rightful place. Her heart fluttered with recognition as she perceived the warmth emanating from the stranger's eyes, a kindness reminiscent of her father's gaze. Hope surged within her, compelling her to cross the distance and seek understanding in the presence of this strange being.

Step by cautious step, she approached the stranger, courage flowing through her veins. Their eyes met, and a genuine smile graced their lips, sending ripples of comfort through her being. Words danced upon her tongue, eager to spill forth like a cascading river, yet before she could voice her bewildered thoughts, the stranger raised a finger to their lips in an unspoken request for silence. A profound stillness descended upon the room as if the very air conspired to shroud their exchange in secrecy. Within her mind, a soft voice reverberated, resonating with timeless wisdom as it whispered the words, "All things in time."

The syllables lingered like an ancient mantra passed down through generations, hinting at the mysterious nature of this sacred sanctuary of knowledge.

She felt coolness on the side of her face. It was refreshing. Somewhere in the distance, voices floated in the air, muffled, as if underwater. She leaned into the coolness, straining. She felt so warm. Her eyes fluttered as she strained to open them. The world was a blur. Golden light and dark shadows.

Slowly, her eyes focused. Morning sunlight streamed through a window. The dark shadows coalesced into a single entity standing over her. She recognized his scarred countenance. Jalin. He stood above her, his left arm outstretched. Was he reaching out to her?

No.

It was his scoring blade. He had pressed its silvered surface against her neck and cheek. Memories of the previous night crashed down upon her.

She was alive.

"I told you she was fine, you arrogant ass!" Esperanza chided.

"Silver is the only reliable… " he began, then stopped when he realized Lyric's eyes were open. He withdrew his blade but continued to eye her cautiously.

"Please stop yelling," she pleaded, beginning to sit up. "I'm fine… " her vision swam, and she reached out to brace herself on the edge of the cot she was laying in. A color she was not expecting caught her eye. Stained white bandages were on her hand. She forced herself to swing her feet over the side of the bed and planted them solidly on the floor. There was something on her throat. Cautious fingers reached to touch the bandages there. She could feel the wound beneath, raw and sore. She turned panicked eyes to Esperanza.

"Blades and claws, not teeth. You are fine," the Voca assured.

She released a breath she did not realize she was holding and nodded.

"What the hell were you thinking?" Jalin asked.

"I'm sorry?" Lyric replied. She blinked and tried to shake the confusion from her head, but the shaking only made it worse.

"You should be." He continued. "You could have been killed… or worse!" he snapped. "I don't care if you are an Imperial Servant. That was reckless!"

Lyric paused, trying to take in Jalin's words. She shook her head again, this time in defiance. "No," she said firmly.

"Excuse me?"

"No. It wasn't." She repeated. She tilted her head upward, foggy eyes searching for the man. "I was doing what needed to be done. Protecting our Voca."

"How dare you… "

"I do dare," Lyric continued. She gathered herself up and pulled up into a standing position. "While YOU were off chasing ghouls, I was doing YOUR job, Inquisitor!"

Esperanza's eyes widened slightly at Lyric's tone. She glanced over at Jalin, who was bristling at the accusation. His face colored red in a combination of anger and frustration. Lyric's eyes focused for a moment on Jalin's face. She raised her right hand and shoved her index finger into his chest.

"You. Weren't. There!" she said with pointed emphasis. Hot tears streamed down her bruised face. "We needed you!" she yelled. "We needed you, and you were chasing an enemy that was already retreating!" She balled up her fists and pounded his chest. "You left us! People were dying! I did what you told me to do!" She hit him in the chest once more. He stood there and took it, jaw tight, fists clenched at his sides.

"I did what you told me… to do… "

Lyric felt salty tears stream down her face. Jalin stood there until her frustration was spent, then raised his hands and carefully wrapped his fingers around her wrists and peeled her fists off of him. He released his grip on her, took a few steps back, and leaned on a small dresser.

The small room was silent for a few moments before Esperanza spoke, "According to the count, the Peacekeeper said there were seven of the creatures and half a dozen ghouls. They are searching for others, but so far they have found nothing. The threat is contained."

Lyric sat back down on her bed and watched Esperanza. The Voca was pale. Her normally fastidious appearance was worn, her hair down, robes tattered and stained with mud and blood. She braced herself on the back of a nearby chair.

"How many of the miners... did we lose?" Lyric asked.

"Maybe a dozen," Jalin replied softly. He cleared his throat and glanced at Esperanza. "I... I need to check on the survivors." Locking the blade back into place, he made his way to the door and opened it, but stood for a moment with his back turned. Lyric watched him and waited, but he said nothing and closed the door behind him without looking back.

The room was again filled with silence.

"He came looking for you," Esperanza said.

Lyric frowned.

"When it was done. You were the first person he came looking for."

Lyric looked down at her bandaged hand. "Oh."

"I am alive because of you. Thank you for that," Esperanza continued. She placed a comforting hand on Lyric's shoulder. "Exhausted and spent but alive."

Lyric opened her mouth to interject. Esperanza cut her off. "It had to be done. What you did. What I did. To save lives. More people are alive because of Hil's gifts. However, there is a cost for magic, and I must accept that. It is my burden and not one you can take the blame for, understand?"

Wordlessly, Lyric nodded her head in forced acceptance. "So, what do we do now?" Lyric asked.

"Cortez wants to head back to the Central Gate. We need to report to the Order," Esperanza said. "We may have a handle on things now, but sending an additional team out to scour the range will be needed, just to be certain."

Lyric nodded her head. "Stone mentioned they had sent messages to Paraíso Verde a month ago asking for help. We need to know what happened to those messengers."

"Yes," Esperanza said, "As soon as Cortez returns from dealing with the injured, we can leave."

Lyric's brow furrowed. "You're the one with healer's training. Why is he with the injured?"

Esperanza's tired eyes were filled with a moment of sadness. "When Jalin came to check on you, he came here first to check on your injuries. He wanted to be sure you were okay … but also to make certain you were not infected. Luckily, the cuts were because of being slammed into the barrier. If you were infected, he would have had to… " She left the sentence unfinished.

Lyric look down at her hand again and then looked up at Esperanza. "The survivors, if any of them are infected… "

Esperanza simply nodded her head. "He will take care of them as well."

HIL'S MOST FAITHFUL

The bright glare of Hil's Grace gave birth to the mother of headaches. Lyric squinted her eyes and tried once more to catch her bearings. Early morning light slowly ate away at the shadows of the land as the cart slowly moved down the road away from Biruji. Each bump and jostle added another stab from some unseen needle that continued to burrow its way into her brain.

She sat in the back of the wagon, curled into one corner, wrapped in blankets guarding against the morning chill of the mountains. Esperanza sat in the driver's seat, carefully driving the horses down the treacherous mountain path, back to Mathis. Lyric wanted to find her notebook and chronicle the events of last night, but the thought of trying to put words to paper made her head swim.

She had felt well, if tired, when she woke that morning. But the more active she was, the more effort it took for her to continue. She had finally stumbled one too many times for Jalin's comfort and he had carried her to the wagon and ordered her to remain in place. She wanted to argue with the man but she was too tired.

"She needs a doctor." She heard Esperanza say.

"I'll have Stone send to Tayler for a report," Jalin responded.

Was the world speeding past her, or trudging through molasses? She could not tell.

In their journey, Jalin's wide-brimmed hat came to rest on her head, shading her eyes from the sun. She blinked and tried to focus but the world swam with blurred vision and nausea. Reaching back, she gingerly felt the large knot at the back of her skull. She winced slightly and sighed.

They had not spoken since their argument. The dour Inquisitor had remained tight-lipped while in her presence, avoiding conversation. She could make out his shape at the end of the wagon now, watching the retreating landscape. His rifle lay in the wagon's bed next to him. Occasionally, he would glance over his shoulder to check on her but said nothing.

If Jalin and Esperanza spoke that morning, Lyric had no memory of it. She vaguely remembered Esperanza guiding her around before she stumbled. The Voca's face was pale and her eyes filled with exhaustion. She had pushed her gift past the limitations, and now her body was paying the balance. Her normal facade seemed warmer but tinged with sadness. Lyric wondered if she caused sadness on the Voca's face.

Esperanza held the reins while Jalin watched the world around them. It was probably the most amicable either

Inquisitor had been to one another. There were no glares or sniping, only the occasional look back from Jalin, who watched her and gave her a nod. While he may not have been talking, he was still looking after her. In his own way.

Silently, she watched the barricade fade into the distance and thought about her childhood. Like all children, she thought about the shadows that moved in the night, fueling the fear of the young mind. Fear of the darkness and its sinister purpose. In the safety of morning, children are often told by adults that El Cucuy and other creatures weren't real despite their fears. They would learn soon enough what did and did not walk the night. Thanks to the Corpse Wars, there were plenty of real monsters walking around the world. Muddling their minds with fears of myths and legends seemed pointless.

Hil's Faithful knew the truth, however. Sometimes legends were real. Kay Stone and the people of Biruji no longer laughed at the notion of childhood fears. They fought against monsters of legend last night. Creatures that existed as only a lesson for others. They were real and killed their friends and terrorized their loved ones.

Lyric thought about the moment that Kay Stone realized that monsters of myth were real. The moment childhood fears became reality. She recalled her time in the Library and carrying locked tomes of information to researchers. She'd wondered why they were locked. Now she understood. Perhaps ignorance was better than confirming the truth of a nightmare.

Perhaps El Cucuy was real...

The wagon came to a stop. Lyric felt the weight of the vehicle shift. No doubt Esperaza and Jalin disembarking. She curled herself deeper into her blankets and the darkness of Jalin's hat and let sleep wrap its welcome arms around her.

Gentle hands. Warm. They helped her into a bed. It was soft and smelled of lavender.

Lyric's eyes fluttered as she tried to open them. Where was she?

The smell of liniment and curatives filled her nose.

A hospital?

"Shhh, just rest for a bit," a familiar voice soothed.

She shook her head.

"Messages... to... deliver... urgent... information... "

"I know. The Inquisitors are here with me now, Lyric."

"Where... "

"You're in Mathis with Doctor Miracle. You've had a head injury. Do you remember?"

She nodded her head. "There was a fight."

"Yes. You have a concussion. I need you to rest," the doctor insisted.

She shook her head once more. "They need... to know... "

"Hush, child, listen to the doctor." Esperanza's voice cut in. "Cortez and I are reviewing the reports from Biruji, Tayler, and Mathis. You can rest while we do that." The Voca's hand pressed gently on Lyric's shoulder, pushing the young woman down, showing she should stay abed.

"Don't leave... without me," the young woman pleaded. She couldn't be left behind at this point. She had to see this through.

"I promise."

Esperanza walked out of the small bedroom where Lyric slept. She wiped her hands on the apron tied around her waist and looked over at the table where Jalin sat. A selection of loose papers and journals covered the space before him.

He glanced up at her briefly and returned to his work.

"Doctor Miracle says she will be fine. Thank you very much." Esperanza quipped. She moved to the stove and the soup pot on its surface. She carefully spooned its dark contents into a bowl. The rich, meaty aroma of venison stew wafted upward.

Jalin nodded and continued reviewing documents.

Esperanza scowled at the man and sat down across from him.

"Don't get soup on the papers," Jalin said absently. He moved a couple of reports out of the way and focused on a third. "It makes no sense."

"Hil's light preserve us, he speaks!" Esperanza said.

Jalin turned irritated eyes on his partner. "We don't have time for this."

"She could have died, Cortez." Esperanza replied, "On her Verdad, and we would have been held accountable."

Jalin watched Esperanza's face a moment and then looked back at the documents. "She knew the risks when she left the Imperial Walls. She could have chosen something else. She chose to venture outside."

"You are impossible."

Jalin closed his eyes and let his head hang for a moment. He exhaled. "No. What I am is realistic." He looked back at his partner. "That young woman will either come out of this experience stronger for it, or will never leave the Imperial Walls again. Either way, she will understand more of what this world truly is, and will have been made safer for it." He reached for a journal and flipped it open. "And not have her head muddled by fantastical stories in books written by people who were never here, romanticizing legends and creating heroes where there are none."

"Is that what this is about?" Esperanza asked. "Because she's an Imperial Scribe? You're concerned about how history will record you now?"

Jalin snapped the notebook closed and jerked his head up to glare at Esperanza. "As well you should be, Voca Boyorquez!" He barked. "There are NO RECORDS on what we encountered last night. NONE. All we have are millennia's worth of oral legends." He paused. His voice lowered as he glanced toward the room where the young Scribe lay. "Those eyes. HER eyes. HER pen. They will be the first to record these creatures in the history of the Inquisition. If we cannot contain this outbreak... those who follow us will rely on her words to guide them." He looked back at Esperanza. "They need to understand the horror of the encounter and the danger of the enemy..." Jalin sucked briefly on his tooth and then went back to his reports. "...and not turn us into something we are not."

She considered him a moment, this rough-hewn slayer of monsters. He was raised by the Temple, as she had been. But his upbringing had been so very different.

"And what are we, Jalin?" she asked quietly.

The answer came without pause or consideration. He did not even look up from the records he reviewed.

"Hil's most faithful."

"Adrenaline, fear, and unconsciousness do not nourish a body, Ms. Wax. You need to eat." Dr. Miracle handed the young woman a cup of warm broth. Her stomach roiled in response.

"I can't."

"Then you stay here until you are recovered and we carry on without you." Jalin interjected from the doorway.

A jolt of cold fire seized Lyric's stomach at the words. She looked at Jalin. "No!"

"Inquisitor Cortez... " Dr. Miracle cautioned. She crossed the room and met the gaze of the man. "Do not manipulate my patient, Inquisitor. I'll not have her bullied into healing. It doesn't work that way."

Jalin sniffed derisively and looked over the Doctor's shoulder. Lyric was sipping from the bowl she had been offered. His gaze drifted back to hers and he gestured toward Lyric with his chin. "And yet… "

Pilar Miracle looked back at the young woman in the bed. Moments earlier, her pallor was green-tinged and her eyes could barely focus. Now her cheeks were flushed and her eyes bright as she slowly but steadily consumed the broth. She narrowed her eyes and glared at Jalin.

"She is concussed and needs rest."

Jalin nodded. "Then," He looked at Lyric. "If Miss Wax agrees… She can rest in the back of the wagon on the way down the mountain. We need to make the Central Gate before nightfall." Without waiting for a reply, he turned and departed.

Pilar inhaled deeply and forced her hands to relax. She turned back to Lyric. "You *can* stay here if you don't feel up to the journey." She crossed back to her and sat on the end of her bed.

A sad smile tugged at Lyric's lips. She set the bowl aside. "I appreciate the offer, Doctor. Truly. But I have to see this through. There is too much at stake."

"Too much at stake? It's just ghouls. You can't live on this side of the Gate and not deal with them, eventually."

Lyric tugged absently at a loose thread on the blanket. "May I ask you a question?"

"Of course."

"Have you ever been certain of a diagnosis, and then, in the middle of the operating theatre, you realized it was a much more complex illness?" she asked.

Pilar considered carefully. "Once or twice, rarely, but even a physician can make the occasional misdiagnosis."

Lyric nodded and listened. "What did you do when you discovered that?"

The doctor inhaled deeply and leaned back a little in thought. "Well, you do the best you can, adjust your treatment plan, and try to save the patient."

Lyric listened and nodded once more. She looked up then and offered Pilar a bittersweet smile. "Adjustments... have been made."

The color drained from Pilar's face. "And the patient?"

"Still on the operating table." She replied cryptically.

"I... see. Is there anything we can do?"

"Can you... help... Esperanza?" she asked cautiously.

Pilar shook her head. "Your Voca's ailment is spiritual, not physical. She has overextended what her body can channel."

"Will she recover, do you think?" Lyric asked with a note of hopeful longing in her voice.

Pilar reached out and patted Lyric's hand. "She is a good woman, and strong in her faith. I am certain Hil would not punish her for wanting to help people. Give her time."

Lyric picked at the blanket some more. "I see. Can you... can you tell Finn I asked about him?"

Pilar smiled. "He and his cousin departed shortly after you did. They had a long trip eastward, apparently."

"Oh?"

"Visiting a traveling researcher who was in the area. A Professor Aberson?"

Lyric's face lit up at the name. "Really?"

"You know him?"

"He's very influential in Scrivener circles. The foremost authority on languages, spoken and written. His most regarded works dealt with deciphering the histories of the Primeras and their legends. Oh, I wish I had known. I would have asked Finn to tell him there's an El EmGee at Paraíso Verde!"

Miracle smiled. "If they make it back this way, I will let Finn know."

Lyric smiled at that. "Thank you, Doctor. I appreciate it."

Pilar stood. She considered a moment and then said, "You just take care of the patient, and... help ensure they make it through."

Lyric looked up at the doctor. Her green eyes were sharp and focused for the first time in what felt like forever.

"I promise."

KEEPER OF LEDGERS

Esperanza's skill with horses helped lessen their time on the trail, and the trek back to the Central Gate from Mathis was smoother with the sun overhead. Their original trip up the mountainside had been filled with cautious turns and slow walking horses. With Hil's light shining brightly, they made quick time down the road, leaving the mining towns and their discoveries behind them.

Lyric remained bundled against the chill in the back of the wagon. She rested as best as she could. Her head ached and her vision still occasionally swam, but the nausea had passed and she was more sure of her footing. She had been lucky and she knew it.

Jalin sat in the back of the wagon with Lyric, his sharp eyes watching the horizon for danger. Occasionally, he broke from his visual scans to review notes in his journal. Invariably he scowled, closed the journal and returned to scanning the mountainside.

Esperanza's weary frame tugged, pulled, clucked, and whistled as the two horses carried them back to civilization.

Two dust and blood-covered Inquisitors, and a young woman in a borrowed Guild cart, converged with the West-bound travelers toward the Great Gates. The foot traffic they encountered on the way back from Mathis came to a standstill outside the Mountain Pass Gates.

"Why have we stopped?" Jalin pulled his eyes off of his notebook and looked around. Seeing the mass of milling people, his countenance darkened.

"Because others are also on the road, Cortez, and they would like to get through the Gates as well." Esperanza sighed.

Lyric watched as the irritation on Jalin's face grew. Had they been traveling with a proper retinue, there would have been a pair of riders followed by a Herald shouting "MAKE WAY FOR THE GLORY OF HIL!" They would have had guards and a standard bearer displaying the sigil of the Inquisition. The display would have immediately called for those around them to part the road and give the followers of Hil a wide berth. If they had a proper retinue, they would have been leaving the Central Gate already and riding out for their next destination.

All they had was Lyric.

She peered out from her blanket bundle at the people of the Imperium on the road with them. There was a haunted look to the eyes of many who dwelt beyond the Walls and Gates that provided safety from the remnants of the Corpse Wars. Growing up in the Capital, she had often wondered at this. After the incidents of the past few days, she now wondered if her own eyes would carry those same shadows.

A flash of green and gold caught Lyric's eye. The badge of a runner!

Flinging the blanket to the side, she forced herself to kneel and lean over the edge of the wagon as her eyes searched the crowd.

"Careful, girl!" Jalin snapped at her unexpected actions. He reached to steady her and keep her from falling over the side.

Scores of dusty bodies in dusky-colored clothes filled the road. In the gathering of people, one stood out. A young man, barely old enough for his own Verdad, carried a board with a sheaf of paper clipped to it. His brilliant green jerkin was like a lighthouse in a storm. He listened to a bald man, nodding and jotting down information.

Lyric glanced back into their wagon, searching for… THERE! Her eyes landed on a basket filled with foodstuffs: the lunch that Doctor Miracle had sent with them.

Nimble fingers quickly snatched the basket and leaned back over the edge of the wagon, eyes searching once more.

Yes!

"Lunch! Lunch for the Runner!" she called out. Her voice carried a melodic sing-song to it. "Lunch! Lunch for the Runner!" she sang again.

Heads turned toward them all.

"What are you doing, Wax?!" Jalin demanded.

She waved him off.

"Lunch! Lunch for the Runner!" Lyric cried out a third time.

The youthful face of the Runner turned toward her voice. She waved the basket back and forth. His eyes widened and a smile spread across his barely bearded face. He threaded his way through the crowd of people. A woman sneered at Lyric and leaned in to say something to the man accompanying her, slapping him on the shoulder and pointing. He nodded apologetically in response.

The young man approached the side of the wagon and quickly assessed the occupants and the wagon. His amber-colored eyes lingered on the Guild sigil on the front of the wagon a moment and then returned to the people in the wagon.

"Destination and business?" the Runner asked.

"Central Gate, Keeper of Ledgers," Lyric replied and offered the basket to him.

He smiled in response, accepting the obvious bribe. "Thank you... wait... who?" his voice cracked.

Lyric gingerly removed part of the bandage on her neck, careful to not expose her injury, and only her tattoo.

The Runner's eyes went wide, and his face a little green, "I... see. Erm... Broken quill?" he asked.

She shook her head. "A little bent, but not broken. We need to see the Master of Ledgers as quickly as possible." She paused and quietly added, "It's about spilled ink."

His eyes widened and, with a quick nod of his head, the Runner took out a bright yellow flag before speeding away toward the gate.

"What was that all about?" Jalin asked as he watched the Runner dart through the crowd, waving his yellow flag high in the air.

Lyric let herself sink back into the back of the wagon as she turned to look at Jalin. "We all have our phrases and codes, Inquisitor." She smiled a little.

"Spilled Ink? Broken Quill?"

Esperanza chuckled as she listened. She glanced over her shoulder at the pair. "He was asking her if she was injured and needed medical attention."

Lyric nodded and lowered her voice. "Spilled Ink means we have lost or missing messages, which could impact multiple Guilds."

"Hmph," Jalin grunted in an almost appreciative response. He glanced back down the road toward the gates. Dozens of faces had turned to look at them. He pursed his lips, grabbed his wide-brimmed hat, and climbed onto the buckboard next to Esperanza. Curious eyes widened at the sight of the man in worn Inquisitorial attire. Whispers floated around them as the crowd slowly stepped away from the wagon and its occupants.

Suddenly, the road exploded into activity. Ahead of them a pair of armed Salon Guards began to shout and bark orders, creating a lane on the on the westbound road. The Runner appeared once more, this time on horseback. He waved them forward.

A blood and dirt-covered pair claiming to be Inquisitors, in a wagon that did not belong to them, carrying an injured Scribe. Curiosity, fear, and respect covered the faces of the people in the crowd as Esperanza drove the wagon through the gates. Salon Guards stood at the ready. Sharp eyes scrutinized the group as they passed.

There were questions that demanded answers.

Lyric glanced skyward at the sunlight and hoped they had time.

Jul Gallegos was the Keeper of Ledgers for the Central Gate. They had done their time as both a Runner and Staffer, but what ultimately gave them the edge was their memory. Jul's brain could track numbers and dates with an unheard-of accuracy. How they had kept that vast amount of knowledge was unknown, even to Jul.

Now, the abilities that helped them attain this position were being questioned by an unproven, disheveled Scribe and her two Inquisitors.

Gallegos sat with a cool look on their face. Whatever annoyance or apprehension they had was unperceivable at the moment. It was a trained look of detachment, honed by years of service in an often thankless position.

Standing next to Jul's desk stood a visibly angered man, Berto Hudson. Hudson was the Officer in Charge of the Messenger Guild for the Central Gate. Like Gallegos, Hudson had climbed his way up within the Guild through dedication and hard work. Unlike Gallegos, Hudson did not hide his irritation. He wore it like a cloak. From the scowl on his face to the sour notes in his tone, there was no mistaking his great displeasure at what was being presented.

Opposite Gallegos sat Lyric Wax. She smiled and nodded, as pleasantly as she had been instructed to do when in the presence of her superiors. When her Verdad was complete, these people would be her colleagues. She wanted to establish the right tone.

Jalin Cortez, however, had no reservations in telling both officers exactly what he thought of them and their procedures. Three separate mining towns had sent messages for aid to the Shrine at Paraíso Verde, and only one had ever reached its destination.

Late.

It had taken the cool hand and calming demeanor of Voca Boyorquez to keep the discussion from devolving into fists and knives. The yellow-clad Voca stood between both men. Her fingers laced and resting above her chest she was a stately figure of tranquility.

Lyric cleared her throat and met the gaze of Keeper Gallegos across the desk. "Apologies Keeper Gallegos and Officer Hudson. The past two days have been... taxing... on the resources of the Inquisition. Exhaustion is high and tempers are short." She shot a look at Jalin, but he and Hudson refused to break eye contact with each other. "Is it possible the missives were sent elsewhere? To another Shrine? Perhaps to one further east of here?"

Jul sighed and stood up. "We are well acquainted with the personage of the... honorable... Inquisitor Jalin Cortez." Jul's eyes drifted to the scoring blade along Jalin's arm. "And have no desire to escalate matters that can be resolved with ink instead of blood."

Jalin relaxed slightly at the words, but his eyes remained on Hudson.

"If I may?" The Keeper gestured to a bookshelf beyond both men, on the other side of Esperanza.

Esperanza smiled warmly at Gallegos and stepped out of the way.

"Blessed Voca," Jul inclined their head to Esperanza as they walked over to a large bookcase. Six shelves contained dozens of ledgers, carefully secured behind glass. The covers of the ledgers varied in color, but appeared to be color coded with ribbons. Gallegos opened the glass doors and removed two volumes with blue ribbons. They returned to their desk and effortlessly thumbed through both large volumes.

Lyric's eyes sharpened with interest. She leaned forward to peer at the words and symbols written there.

"These are the records for all messages received by this office for the last two calendar months." Jul turned the ledger around and pointed at a specific set of lines.

"As you can see here, the first message within the time you note was dropped off by an M. Crum... a local of Mathis acting as a courier as there is no formal Guild presence there. That message was recorded by the Central Gate from Mathis exactly two months and 6 days ago, at 12:02 in the afternoon."

Lyric leaned over to examine the ledger.

"Inquisitor?" she said to Jalin. "Perhaps you would like to compare notes?" she asked softly.

Jalin narrowed his eyes at Hudson one more time and then finally broke away from their silent stand-off. He reached into the pocket of his vest and pulled out his notebook, then flipped through it several times.

"It is noted here as a specific line entry because it was outside of the normal time frame of bulk missives from those communities. The message was accepted by Clerk W. Perez, released to the Messenger Guild for delivery to the Paraíso Verde Shrine."

Jalin placed his notebook next to the ledger to compare his own notes taken from the Peacekeeper logs of Tayler, Biruji, and Mathis.

"The time of release to the Guild Messenger was 2:16 in the afternoon. Upon their return, the Messenger noted delivery by the Guild courier at 8:49 in the evening, signed for by the Shrine Paraíso Verde."

"How are these deliveries confirmed if you are not there?" Jalin asked as he continued to examine the ledger.

"We take the Courier's signature logs when they return and they are copied over, then returned to the Courier," Gallegos replied.

"Standard Guild procedure, Inquisitor," Lyric confirmed.

"But they *could* be forged?" Jalin asked.

Hudson bristled at the perceived insult, shoulders back and neck stretching.

Jul paused a moment before answering. "Courier logs from Shrines are typically sealed with a signet stamp, which is compared and verified. Unless the signet seal for Paraíso Verde has fallen into questionable hands, I find it doubtful they were forged."

"Noted. Please continue," Jalin commented.

"Thirteen days later, a second missive specifically addressed to the Shrine at Paraíso Verde was received." Jul pointed at another line of entry. "Dates, times, and chain of custody are all shown here. I'm showing seven messages received from Mathis. The two that were initially received and the third through sixth, which were labeled as urgent and carried with them the Peacekeeper's seal. The seventh entry... here... was a pair of missives, both with the Peacekeeper seal. One was addressed to the same shrine and the other to Sanctuary in the Capital. That was as of four days ago."

Jalin looked up at Esperanza at the comment. "The Temple at Sanctuary has been alerted."

Esperanza's shoulders relaxed at the words, and her forced smile faltered slightly. "Then aid is on the way." Her fingers brushed across the golden sun sigil at her throat.

Jalin tugged a folded missive out of his notebook and handed it to Gallegos. "Was this the message that was sent from here to Paraíso Verde four days past?"

Jul accepted the letter and looked through the note. Nodding, they flipped it over and assessed the back of the missive. Though the seal was faded, the ink stamped into the back was still legible to the Keeper's eyes.

"Yes, the Central Gate and the Messenger Guild's sigils can still be seen here and there." They pointed to two faded images: a pair of towers divided by a mountain, and the ever-present scorpion of the Guild. "This was received and processed here. Based on the date written within, this was the most recent one."

Jalin nodded and considered the note for a moment. He glanced at Lyric, and then at Esperanza. The Voca took a deep, resigned breath and turned a forced smile to the Keeper.

"We respectfully request to speak to the Messenger in charge of the Paraíso Verde run."

SPILLED INK

R unners delivered messages within the safety of city
walls. They were attached to the Imperial Library and
served at the whim of the Grand Librarian. They handled
personal messages and deliveries within the confines of
their assigned cities and stations.

The Guild handled messages, cartage, and cargo outside
the confines of city walls. They were trained to handle horses
and carts, long distances, and to defend themselves while
on the road. Messengers were a close-knit group of people
who knew how to rely upon themselves. Beyond the safety of
city walls, there was rarely anyone to call upon for help.

Over the centuries, the Guild had crafted a complete
atlas of serviceable roads, paths, and routes throughout
the Imperium. They established a network of way stations
and safe houses to ensure the security of their messengers,
cargo, and charges. The persons who signed on with The
Guild understood they would probably die performing the
service they had sworn to.

And they did not appreciate having their methods questioned.

Rinaldo Cantu was a stocky man with a balding pate and patchy beard. He was broad and thick and often smelled of bacon grease and old cheese. He stepped inside the Office of the Keeper of Ledgers, removed his hat, and nodded to everyone present. His eyes surveyed the occupants quickly and then landed on Officer Hudson. Cantu quirked an eyebrow at his Guild representative. Hudson gestured with a silent nod to Keeper Gallegos. Cantu pursed his lips and turned to face the Keeper of Ledgers.

"You asked to see me, Keeper?"

"Mr. Cantu, you make Paraíso Verde run; is that correct?" Gallegos asked.

"Yes, Keeper, as of last month since Gonzalez quit," Cantu said.

"Why did they quit?" Jalin asked from the corner of the room.

Cantu looked over the Inquisitor with scrutiny, and then looked at Hudson and Gallegos, "Uh, who is this?"

Jalin bristled at the insolence of the man. Lyric noted his stance and quickly interjected, "There is an ongoing investigation, Messenger Cantu. When was the last time you were in Paraíso Verde?"

"That ain't none of your business, girly." Cantu shot back. "Who are these people?" he asked, looking at Hudson.

"These 'good' people believe you haven't been doing your job, Messenger. According to them, the missives meant for the Shrine in Paraíso Verde are two months missing," Hudson said with a slight smile of malice.

Cantu sniffed and turned hard eyes on Lyric. "That. Is. Horseshit." he swore. He took a step toward her. "My books are always accurate and my runs are clean! Who the hell do you think you are, questioning a Guild Messenger?!" he demanded. "We put our lives on the line every day to ensure things get delivered!"

The bandage on the side of Lyric's neck was loose. The ink of her Imperial tattoo was visible. Spying the tattoo on her neck, Cantu's eyes narrowed. He stared at it and then back at her.

"Oh, I get it, now." He pulled his shoulders back and took another step toward her. "You think because you bear the Throne's mark, you can do whatever the hell you want! This Imperium runs on this Guild's dedication. Not sitting behind some desk and complaining about the timeliness of our service." He stood before her, looking down at her.

She met his eyes, unwavering. Behind her, she heard the sound of leather stretching. In her head, she could see Jalin's form tense in anticipation of violence.

"Oh, whatcha gonna do over there, Flaco?" Cantu said, looking at Jalin. Disdain dripped from his words.

Lyric turned around to see Jalin's face darken. The fingers of his left hand twitched. There was only so much polite discourse he could be expected to entertain. That limit had been reached. From the corner of her eye, she saw Hudson moving forward as well.

Cantu's lips pulled back into a lopsided sneer. "You wanna take a swing at me?" He asked Jalin.

Jalin stretched his neck.

Cantu looked back at Lyric. "No? How about you?" he held up a meaty finger in front of her face. "A Scribe with no words? Huh." He pointed his finger at her and poked her collarbone.

"How...," poke, "about," another poke, "you."

Before Cantu's finger could connect with Lyric's collarbone a third time, she reached up and seized it with her right hand. Grasping his finger, she pushed it up and backward toward his wrist. As he screamed in unexpected agony and fell to his knees, she twisted and stepped behind the man, pulling his helpless arm toward the roof.

Holding his arm aloft, Lyric stated in a calm voice, "Mr. Cantu, a Servant of the Throne does not need a member of the Inquisition to fight their battles for them. Like yourself, I have been trained in self-defense." With a flick of her wrist, she threw his hand away from her grasp.

Cantu gasped in pain once more.

She looked across the room at Officer Hudson. "Do. Not. Test. Me."

Keeper Gallegos smirked a little and folded their arms across their chest.

The young woman tugged at the hem of her jerkin to regain her lost composure. "Apologies," she said to the Keeper of Ledgers. "We have spent the last 48 hours clearing a ghoul infestation in Tayler, Mathis, and Biruji."

Gallegos and Hudson's expressions changed to shock.

"What?!" they both demanded.

"And fighting to save the lives of those townships." she continued. "The Inquisitors are exhausted, but they still have jobs that need doing… just as we do." Lyric looked down at Cantu's greasy face. "We need to determine the extent of the infection."

Cantu nodded. Cradling his hand, he carefully climbed back up to a standing position.

Clearing her throat, she asked, "Mr. Cantu, can you please tell us what happened to the last messenger?"

Cantu glanced over to Hudson, who simply nodded. "Nancy Gonzalez walked off the job. It's rare that it happens, but it does from time to time. Some people aren't about this life. We'd figured Nancy met someone on the job and decided that she was done."

Hudson added, "When a driver is a no-show, we send out a team of two to investigate. In this case, they found her wagon in Paraíso Verde proper. The horses were hitched, and the wagon was fine. There was no sign of trouble or violence, and according to the locals, Nancy made all the deliveries. We brought the wagon back and checked it out, nothing out of the ordinary. With no witnesses and no violence, we left her information with the Peacekeeper in Verde in case she shows up."

Jalin looked to Lyric and Esperanza and then back to Hudson. "When was this?"

"Shy of two months. She would have been the one who delivered the first two messages to the Shrine you were asking about," Jul said.

"And I've been delivering the rest," Cantu added.

"Has Luz Wheeler already briefed you on the situation in Paraíso Verde?" Lyric asked.

"What situation?" Hudson asked. "Wheeler's not been back through since... " he paused, "Since driving you lot out to Verde... "

Lyric felt an empty sensation in her stomach but forced herself to proceed. "She loaned us her wagon when we left the Shrine two days ago. She was supposed to alert the local farms to a possible infection and to stay out of Paraíso Verde. We assumed she would have made it back here by now."

The blank looks and shaking heads from the Keeper and two Guild members cemented her fear. Before she could speak, she heard Esperanza clear her voice. The Voca had been quiet throughout the entire scene. Lyric assumed she was trying to conserve her strength.

"Two days ago, we came to Paraíso Verde on a regularly scheduled delivery for the Verde Shrine. We arrived early morning to find the remains of the town proper destroyed. Partially burned, buildings caved in. Rampant destruction. We found no soul alive there. And found no bodies. The Shrine was the only other inhabited area that we were aware of. We traveled out to the Shrine and spoke with our contact there. He alerted us to an issue in Mathis. He indicated a message had arrived a few days earlier. He made no mention of any other requests for aid, or missives from Mathis, Tayler, or Biruji. Messenger Wheeler was gracious enough to let us use the wagon to investigate. She took a pack animal from the Shrine and departed to alert the local farms of the tragedy." Esperanza paused and inhaled a slow, meditative breath. "It is obvious she never made it back to The Gates... which does not bode well."

Jalin recovered the original missive from Gallegos' desk and held it aloft. He looked at Cantu. "Other than the two that were delivered by Gonzalez, you delivered all the recent missives to Verde Shrine?"

"Yeah... yeah," he nodded. "Same guy signed off on all the ones I dropped off," Cantu said. "His name should be in the record book."

Jalin nodded. "Can you describe him?"

Esperanza glanced at Jalin. "Do you think someone signed for the missives and destroyed them?"

"I'm discounting nothing at this point," he replied and then looked back at Cantu.

"Older fella, a mix of gray and white hair and bright blue eyes. He was probably..." he sized Jalin up a moment, "Four or five inches taller than you. Big guy. He said his name was... Carson, Levi Carson," Cantu replied. Cantu's eyes focused on Jalin's exposed hands and the ink tattoos that covered them. "He also had marks like yours, a bit faded... but essentially the same."

Jalin's eyes narrowed. " I think you must surely be mistaken, Messenger Cantu. The man with these tattoos, who is at Verde Shrine, is in a Mechanist chair."

Cantu shook his head."Sir, I may be many things, but I know my job. This guy... Carson... took the messages from me. He had that same tattoo on the back of his hand. He wasn't in any kind of chair, and he was standing as well as anyone. There was no one else that answered, and it was always this guy Carson, regardless of the time of day."

The blood drained from Jalin's face at those words. The Manos looked over at his partner and then to Lyric. Nodding to himself, he slowly folded the missive back up and wordlessly tucked it inside his vest. He turned and exited the room.

Lyric watched Jalin depart, then turned to Gallegos, "Keeper, thank you for your time and information. Officer Hudson, and Mr. Cantu... thank you. Please advise travelers to avoid Paraíso Verde for now, until this matter is resolved. You will also want to alert the Salon Guard to secure the Gates and double inspections. Above all else, approve no travel orders to Paraíso Verde. No one goes that way, or to Verde Shrine."

Gallegos nodded. "I will let people know to avoid the area for the time."

Esperanza turned tired eyes to Officer Hudson. She offered a worn smile. "With your leave, Officer Hudson, we would like to continue the use of the wagon."

Hudson pulled his focus back to the Voca. He cleared his throat a little. "Technically, it belongs to the Guild Officer that Luz Wheeler worked under. If it was delegated to you by Wheeler, it's still yours to maintain."

Esperanza nodded quietly. She reached into a pocket within her robes and produced what appeared to be a metal coin. A golden sun was stamped on one side of its surface. The sigil of the Inquisition on the other. She set it on the Keeper's desk.

"I need to send a message, please. It will require your fastest messengers from here to Sanctuary. I need you to tell them that this comes from Esperanza Boyorquez, Voca de Hil. Have them take this icon and tell them... darkness has fallen on Hil's House in Paraíso Verde."

Gallegos eyed the coin on the desk and then reached for pen and paper. He carefully penned the phrase that Esperanza quoted.

"If you are not going to Sanctuary, then where are you all going?" Hudson asked.

"The Shrine, Mr. Hudson," Esperanza said grimly, "To finish this."

SIX MILES

R oad traffic from the West side of the Gates headed in from the Open Lands and The Reach was always busier during the daylight hours. Travelers crowded together, trying to get through the Gates for safety from the Open Lands...

The Western Imperium, the lands West of the Vargas, still suffered deeply from the effects of the Corpse Wars. Packs of ghouls still roamed the area, ghosts haunted crossroads, and Ladies in White pulled passersby into the watery depths as they sought their missing children.

The road from the Gates to Paraíso Verde was a safe route. Travelers could make the journey from the Gates to the Shrine in only a few hours. The Valley there was protected.

Until now.

Lyric and Luz Wheeler had left the Gates and entered unfamiliar territory a few days ago. Now she watched as Runners helped register travelers, noting where they were coming from and where they were headed to and wondered, *How widespread were the remnants of the War? How many of these people faced danger every night? Did they have the help they needed from the Imperium?*

Her journey was supposed to have been a simple errand to an area known for its safety. An opportunity for her to see the world beyond the Gates, talk with the people, and come home to the Imperial Library. Her Prueba, her search for truth, had shown her so much more than she had ever imagined.

As she approached the wagon Luz had loaned them, she spied Jalin sitting in the back, lanky legs draped over its edge. The muzzle of his rifle was visible where it lay next to him. His wide-brimmed hat obscured his scarred face from view, but she could see that he was reading his journal.

He did not look up, "Miss Wax."

"Inquisitor." she replied. They had not really spoken since the incident in Biruji. Her head still ached dully from being flung into the barricade, but she was recovering.

"Voca Boyorquez?" he asked.

"Will be along shortly," she answered. "She is sending to Sanctuary for support."

He nodded. "A wise action." He closed his journal and looked at the sky, then held his hand up to gauge the sun. His lips pursed. "A fast horse runner at full speed will make the Eastern Gate in less than an hour, and Sanctuary another after that, if they have a fresh horse. We'll see support from Haven outside of the Eastern Gate before a retinue from Sanctuary can be here in time."

"In time for what?"

Jalin lowered his hand and stared at Lyric. There was an indignation in Jalin's coffee-colored eyes she had not seen before. It spoke of determination married with destruction.

"In time to help eliminate whoever is impersonating a Hand of Hil."

The sounds of booted feet crunching on the ground behind her stopped Lyric's reply. She glanced over her shoulder to see Esperanza. The Voca's face was worn, her complexion washed out and pale.

Jalin frowned and pushed off the back of the wagon to stand. He stepped up to the Voca and examined her face, then nodded.

"You're in the back. Wax, you're driving," he stated with finality. He turned and lifted Esperanza into the back of the wagon.

Lyric balked, "What?!"

"You'll be fine," Esperanza said as she curled up next to the driver's seat in the back of the wagon. "They are Guild horses. They are an experienced team. It's a known road… and I will be right here if you need me."

Lyric took a deep breath. "My quest does not end here…" she said solemnly and mounted the wagon to take her seat.

Under Esperanza's guidance and instructions, Lyric took the reins and urged the horses forward. Part of her wanted the horses to sprint toward the Shrine, but Lyric knew she did not know enough to control them if something happened. She looked over her shoulder at the back of the wagon. Esperanza was curled in the bed under the driver's seat, where she was sheltered in shade from the sun. Jalin sat cross-legged at the rear gate, his hands resting on his knees. He silently watched the horizon as they traveled, thoughts consuming him.

It was a strange reflection compared to how they were a few days ago. It seemed forever ago. The events of the last few days had changed them all. There was no tension, irritation, or stand-offish behavior from the pair now. There was nothing except exhaustion and gloom.

Gallegos had supplied the wagon with canteens of water, a light meal for the road, and a much-needed sunhat for the young Scribe. Her concussed head was not the only injury she suffered on this journey. Her fair skin was also a victim of the extended out-of-doors that she was unaccustomed to. Dr. Miracle had provided her with a small container of salve used by the locals to help prevent sunburn. It was made from various oils and a few minerals from the local mines. It soothed Lyric's skin and helped prevent additional damage. Now she pulled the brim of the hat down to shade as much of her face as possible as they traveled westward once more, into the afternoon.

About an hour into the ride, she handed out the lunches and canteens that Gallegos supplied. Jalin woke Esperanza enough to ensure the Voca took some water and let her return to her rest. He then resumed his position in the wagon's rear, watching the horizon once more. Lyric thought to engage Jalin in conversation during the trip, but his visage discouraged conversation. His normally sour expression was simply tired now. She hoped he was trying to puzzle through the situation, but feared he was not.

A man calling himself Levi Carson had met with Cantu at each delivery. Presumably, the same person had met Nancy Gonzalez before she walked off the job but there was no way to confirm that unless they could find her. Cantu described the man he met as being healthy and robust. They had seen no sign of anyone matching that description upon their arrival. Indeed, Judex Stonebridge said he had been expecting Brother Carson when their own group had arrived.

Stonebridge did not match the description of the man that Cantu met. Gale Stonebridge was a slip of a man, long past his prime and now confined to a Mechanist's Life Support Chair.

Yet Cantu had described Carson as having the same tattoos on his hands that Cortez wore. The sigils of his office. The mark of an Inquisitor.

Was Carson impersonating Stonebridge?

What if Carson had killed Gonzalez and replaced Stonebridge?

Lyric shook her head. No. Jalin would have recognized the exchange. The way he spoke to Stonebridge. The obvious deference shown. Stonebridge's eases of conversation with Jalin. They knew each other. The mannerisms lent one to believe Stonebridge was a mentor, or perhaps a father figure, to Cortez. Jalin would have seen through the impersonation in an instant.

Unless...

Lyric paused in thought a moment, trying to remember an exchange. Something she had overheard a few days before she departed on Verdad. The Queen of the Reach,

Marisol, had been murdered, and a doppelgänger had been discovered in her place.

Could a shape-changer have replaced the Judex? To what end?

Lyric looked back at Cortez and then back at the road ahead of them. If Gale Stonebridge had been slain and a shape-changer had taken his place...

Jalin would come unhinged.

"Six miles."

Lyric looked up at the darkening sky and then at Jalin.

"Are you certain?"

The Inquisitor scanned the sky once more. A flash of lightning crackled overhead. He counted.

"1-2-3-4-5 ..." as he began to say six thunder rumbled. "Six seconds from the flash to the sound. It's about six miles out."

The storm had moved in from the north about an hour ago. The bright blue sky clouded over, obscuring the warmth of the sun. Slowly the clouds changed from white to gray, and now a deep gray-green. The horses jerked at their reins, causing Lyric to halt the cart and consult with Jalin.

A cool breeze washed over them. Jalin inhaled deeply.

"Rain." He scanned the skies once more. "We need to get under cover before this breaks." He looked up at Lyric. "You're done, Wax. We need a proper driver now." He extended his foot forward and tapped Esperanza's shoe a few times. The Voca opened her eyes and slowly sat up.

"La tormenta," Jalin said and nodded at the sky.

Esperanza shook the sleep from her head. "Understood." she said and pushed herself out of the blankets and into a standing position.

"I'm sorry to wake you, but we have a storm coming and I don't think I can manage them through this," Lyric said.

Esperanza nodded her head. "No, it's fine, child. Managing horses through a storm requires a more experienced hand. How far away are we?" she asked of Jalin.

"Half an hour, maybe a little longer," came the reply.

Settling into the seat, Esperanza instructed Jalin and Lyric to secure themselves. She accepted the reins and gave a small whistle before giving a snap to the reins. The horses responded accordingly and picked up the pace, going faster than before.

As the cart raced against the oncoming storm, Lyric wondered at the woman seated next to her. The image of the living light of Hil within the woman next to her was awe-inspiring and yet, it scared her. Thinking about the light she saw within Esperanza, she also remembered the Voca's words about the fragility of the mortal frame. Human bodies were not meant to bear the spark of the divine, much less control it. When would that cell of flesh and bone fail to hold the power within her? What would happen?

The full face of the storm had not overtaken them by the time the Shrine was within view. Gusts of chill wind pressed against them. The air was heavy with the threat of rain.

Around them, the tall grass danced like a violent green sea. Angry waves rippled across the sea of blades, making the lonely Shrine all the more uninviting.

In the distance, Lyric could see the same Shrine they had visited just days prior. The horses suddenly started to slow and jerk at their reins once more. Esperanza pulled them up and to a stop. The darkened skies clashed with the white walls of the building. Dancing shadows gave it a forbidding appearance.

"What's the issue?" Jalin asked.

"There's something in the air that has them spooked."

Jalin frowned and scanned the area ahead of them. Scowling, he reached inside his long coat and pulled out a spyglass. He placed it against his right eye and searched. A sound like a mix between clearing his throat and a growl emanated from him. Handing the glass to Esperanza, he turned around and started loading up the long guns and pistols.

Esperanza proceeded to view and gave a slight gasp, "Are those... they still look like they are moving!"

"They are," he replied gruffly.

"What's moving? What's going on?" Lyric asked.

Esperanza handed her the spyglass. "On the hillside. Look for the dark spots."

The Scribe's eyes tried to focus on the darkened objects that Esperanza indicated. It looked like charred areas of earth and grass. She adjusted the focus. There was an odd shape in the center of each burned patch. The shapes seemed familiar...

"Hil's light preserve us, are those people?!" Lyric exclaimed. She lowered the glass from her eye, "We need to help them!"

"I don't think those are people anymore," Esperanza said grimly.

"No..." Lyric whispered.

She stared once more at the blackened bodies. One or two of them seemed to move weakly. A human surely would have been dead already, but a vampyre... Lyric recalled the screams of the creatures from the warehouse as fire ripped through them, and then Esperanza's light silencing them. There had only been four then, and their screams had been deafening and destructive.

Half a dozen charred bodies dotted the hillside. Their screams would have been monstrous. Without the light of Hil to destroy them, it might have been possible for them to survive.

"I don't understand. The one that was set on fire went wild before the Voca put them all down. How are they held fast?" Lyric asked.

"Probably staked to the ground. Could be iron spikes," Jalin answered matter-of-factly. "I'm guessing they have been dismembered in some fashion. They've been crippled so they can be finished off later. It's a warning."

Lyric shot a look back to Jalin. "A warning?"

It was Esperanza who answered, "There was a time when the Order felt that there was a need for a public display of justice. It isn't done anymore, and under the current Imperator, it is an outlawed practice."

She looked at Esperanza and, for the first time, Lyric saw a hint of shame in the woman's face. Lyric knew the reputation of the Order was laced with fear and intimidation, but such a display was cruel if not horrifying.

Before she could say anything, movement caught Lyric's attention. At first, she thought it was the flicker of shadows from the lightning. Taking up the spyglass again, she focused on the shadows. They were running along the side of the building! A trio of bodies, and were scaling up the side of the Shrine's walls.

"Jalin, Eastern wall," she said, handing the spyglass over and pointing.

Cortez stared at her for a moment before Lyric realized she had used his given name. Saying nothing, he took the spyglass out of her hand and gazed silently before uttering, "Those walls have no handholds. They are crawling up like spiders."

"What is the plan, Cortez?" Esperanza asked, as she watched the shadows crest and go over the wall.

Jalin chewed on the inside of his cheek for a moment and then nodded to himself. "Going through the front door is not an option. There was a storage cellar, wasn't there? For dry good delivery to the kitchen?"

Esperanza nodded. "Interior and exterior lifts, yes."

"If they haven't gone through the storage cellar, we may be able to go below and come up from there into the kitchen. Bring us around and we'll see what our options are," he said.

Esperanza urged the horses forward as they made a wide path around the Shrine's base. On the northwestern side of the hill, Lyric saw a pair of large wooden doors built into the side of the berm. The doors were wide enough to allow a wagon to enter and were ten feet high. This was the delivery entrance.

Large, heavy, wrought-iron gates protected the doors from the exterior. Some of the bars were mangled and twisted outward, but the gates remained closed. As they approached, Lyric noted the surface of the wood was adorned with delicate carvings. A scene of the valley was carved into the wood. Now much of the design was marred with fist size dents into the wood and deep slashes to its surface.

"Looks like they couldn't get in," Lyric commented.

Esperanza stopped the wagon near a hitch. Jalin climbed out to head toward the door and examined the twisted iron gates.

"You won't find a keyhole, Cortez," Esperanza said. "Place your thumb on the sun and move it to the right and then up. You will hear a click, then let it go. Then press it in again, move it to the left and up. It will click again and unlock."

Jalin nodded and did as instructed as Lyric quickly gathered their belongings. An audible click was heard, and then a second. The sky rumbled deeply overhead. With the metal gates unlocked, Jalin pulled the right side open.

While the massive wooden doors did not have any handles, a few of the decorative carvings actually disguised a pair of handholds. Placing his hands on the holds, he slowly pulled the heavy doors back.

A cough of air from the sealed chamber carried a mixture of body musk and foulness. The unexpected scent of rot caught them off guard and caused a momentary urge to retch. Jalin pulled the other door open in an attempt to release the fetid air.

Turning back to the two women, Jalin put a finger over his lips and quietly unlocked his scoring blade. With solemn nods, the three ventured into the darkness.

CARASIN

A thick gloom accompanied the cloying stench that filled the air. The scent, while disagreeable, was not as intense as the graverot of ghouls. This was the putrid smell of death, decay, and pain.

Lyric followed quietly behind Esperanza and Jalin as they crept through the service entrance. She glanced at the floor periodically, half-expecting it to be caked in something unspeakable. There was only brickwork, though, painstakingly laid by hand a generation past.

Jalin hissed softly and gestured for them to stop. The tunnel opened ahead and lights flickered warmly. They flattened themselves along the wall, out of sight. Cortez peeked around the corner into the room.

"Madre de Dios!" he swore.

"Cortez?" Esperanza asked. She looked past him. A horrified gasp escaped the Voca's lips.

Lyric looked between the two Inquisitors, registering their responses. Her eyes slid toward the room.

"Wax, no!" Jalin exclaimed. He stepped to interpose himself between the young woman and what lay beyond.

Too late.

For once in the young Scribe's life, Lyric Wax wished to unsee the world.

Human physiology was a course all students were expected to take at the University. It was an in-depth study of the human body and all its components. Cadavers were supplied for lessons. Those pursuing medical arts worked directly with them. Lyric spent a chill Autumn one year providing sketches for one resident. She had seen more than many ever would that Fall.

Those images paled compared to what lay before her now.

Three human-shaped iron cages were tucked away in the shadows. They were not empty.

Bodies... bodies on examining tables. Tilted examining tables. Secured with tight leather straps or chains. Three bodies. Two women. One man. Clergy. Chests rose and fell ever so slightly, barely alive. Rubber tubes jutted from veins. Wine red liquid dripped into glass jars. They were being systematically drained!

Lyric's bile rose angrily but she made herself continue to look at the gruesome scene. Among the examination tables, two stood apart from the others, each bearing the weight of a restrained person secured by heavy iron chains. Grim contraptions kept their mouths pried open with thick metal horse bits. As Lyric gazed upon the scene, a sense of familiarity washed over her as she recognized the procedures being conducted on one of them — an autopsy was underway. Above the lifeless form sharpened silver scalpel hung suspended by twine, poised perilously close to the exposed heart.

Lyric pulled her eyes away, glancing at the second figure. Her breath caught in her throat as her chest constricted in grief.

Strapped to the other table was Luz Wheeler. Her skin was gaunt, her complexion pallid and slick. She was supposed to have brought others back to the Shrine for safety!

"No... " Lyric sobbed. She stepped forward to reach for her friend. A hand gripped her shoulder and held her in place.

As she glanced back, she saw Jalin standing there, his hand resting on her shoulder. The index finger of his other hand gestured silently to his mouth. With trepidation, Lyric turned her attention to the woman in front of her once more. Her heart sank into her stomach as she forced herself to gaze into the woman's open mouth. To her horror, rows of sharp fangs were pushing their way through the flesh of the upper jaw. Luz had transformed into one of them... a vampyre.

Jalin gave Lyric a gentle tug and motioned for her and Esperanza to follow him back into the darkness of the tunnel and, eventually, outside.

The cold wind struck Lyric's face, causing her to collapse onto the grass as she was overcome with nausea. The unsettling combination of smells—the chilling air and the distressing situation—, combined with her concussion, compelled her to empty the contents of her stomach. After regaining some composure, she glanced up to find Jalin pacing back and forth, while Esperanza's eyes remained fixed on the door.

Quietly, Lyric asked, "It looked like... some of them... were still alive." She whispered as tears welled up in her green eyes.

Jalin said nothing and continued to pace.

Esperanza turned her attention away from the door. "Those cages were Confessor's Boxes, Cortez," she said coolly. "Someone muzzled those people. Someone knows exactly what those things are and has them secured properly. The creatures... on the tables... they are alive, Cortez, and being sliced open like experiments!"

Jalin stopped and faced her. "I know."

"What's a Confessor's Box?" Lyric asked.

Jalin met Esperanza's gaze, then glanced back at Lyric.

"Rooting out heresy and danger is not a task for the weak of heart, nor is it clean," Jalin answered. He stared down at Lyric as she knelt on the grass, tears staining her exhausted face. He offered her his hand and helped her stand.

"The boxes were once used to... hmmm... ensure accurate information was shared."

"You mean they were coerced?" Lyric answered.

"As you say," Jalin replied. "The practice was outlawed some time ago."

"Then where did they come from?"

"An excellent question."

"Cortez... " Esperanza cut in.

"Ask your question, witch," he spat.

Esperanza flinched slightly at the venom in the slur. "Are you positive the man you saw in the Mechanist chair was Gale Stonebridge?"

Jalin was silent for a few seconds. "Yes."

"What put him in that chair?" she continued.

Jalin hesitated for a moment but answered, "Arrows dipped in Carasin."

Esperanza paused at that, then added, "You know, as well as I do, Carasin is a death sentence, Cortez. Even if they had cut out the infected organs, the poison would still work its way into the bloodstream and into the brain," she said.

The fine line of civility that Jalin had been maintaining snapped. "Do you think he's capable of that madness!?" he said, pointing at the tunnel. "No! He can't live without that damned chair! The amount of work necessary to... the amount of physical labor! No! That's impossible!" He stalked toward her. "Carasin degrades the faculties over time, yes. But that... in there... is not the work of a debilitated mad man. He should have been dead already, but he REFUSED to die because he is a fighter! He may not have been BLESSED by Hil, but he is STILL HERE. And that means Hil has been at his side!" he snarled at her. His breath was ragged and his eyes were wide with emotion.

"When did he retire as Judex?" she prodded softly.

"What difference does that make?"

"Can you be certain it was him in that chair?" she pressed.

"How DARE YOU WITCH!" he growled. His arm tensed. His scoring blade snicked out toward her.

Esperanza lifted her chin to stare him directly in the eye, unabashed and unafraid.

"When did your father retire, Inquisitor Cortez?" Lyric's gentle voice asked.

Jalin snapped his gaze at Lyric. His eyes were full of shock and rage.

"You test a line that should not be tested," he cautioned her.

Lyric carefully stepped between Esperanza and Jalin. Her heart pounded in her ears. "When did Gale Stonebridge retire as Judex?"

Jalin stared at Lyric standing before him. Tear stains on her face. Blood stains on her jerkin. A broken visage of the young woman she was three days earlier when she had been entrusted to his care.

She is your priority.

He closed his eyes and stood silently for a moment before speaking.

"Five... maybe six months ago." He stood still as the breeze blew colder and the sky rumbled overhead. His eyes opened and he stared down into Lyric's face with unshed tears he refused to let go.

"Jalin... "

It began to drizzle. The tears that had welled up in Jalin's eyes were lost as the water fell from the heavens. They stood silently.

"What is the plan, Manos Cortez?" Esperanza said.

Looking up to the gray skies, Jalin took a deep breath and then exhaled. "The plan is the same. We enter there quietly. We will need to bring the horses into the tunnel. You and I will ascend up the freight elevator. Wax will watch the horses," he said and then turned to Lyric. "If we are not back within the hour - ride back to the Central Gate and... "

"I cannot, Cortez," Esperanza said quietly.

"What are you talking about?" he said, confused.

Esperanza rolled up the sleeve of her robe. Running up her arm was a series of inked icons sacred to her faith. Symbols of divine power. Marring these carefully chosen emblems were dark branching lines, reminiscent of the scarring on a tree after a lightning strike. They ran up her arm and into her robe. Hints of those same lines peered out from along the edges of Esperanza's collar. Soft light seemed to glow and pulse in some lines.

Jalin stared at the lines and then back at Esperanza. "How long?"

"Since Biruji. I had hoped rest would settle them." She rolled her sleeve down. "I am spent, Cortez, and we do not have time for me to recover. The power will kill me if I attempt to access it like this... and we need to see this through," she said.

"Then what will you do if I fail?" he asked her solemnly.

Esperanza looked between Jalin and Lyric. "If you BOTH don't return within the hour, I will use this," she said and pulled out a small silver vial.

Jalin's eye twitched as he recognized it immediately. "You've had that on your person this whole time?"

"The Manos have their ways, the Vocas do as well," she said. "If you fail, I will ensure this blasphemy is destroyed and takes whomever or whatever is doing it with me."

Jalin looked at the Scribe, but Lyric just nodded her head. "She's right. We need to see this through."

Jalin returned the nod. "Let's go."

Through diligence and, perhaps, the blessing of Hil, the three brought the horses indoors without disturbing the creatures in the cages. The presence of the trio caused only a slight stir, and those who could see them simply observed in silence. It was as if their time in bondage and suffering had trained them to remain quiet. The eerie sensation made Esperanza uneasy as she settled onto a nearby stool, watching Jalin hand the silvered blade to Lyric. Although she felt a tinge of shame, she knew that her current condition was beyond her control. Ever since they left the mining towns, her body had been plagued by pain and covered in scars that were trying to consume her entirely. The only remedy was rest, time, and Hil's mercy. She had pushed the boundaries of her divine power, abusing it in Biruji to bring down the dangerous Milagro—an act that had been necessary. If she had allowed the Milagro to flow through her for a second longer, it would have been fatal. She would never admit this to Jalin.

Her attention shifted to the young woman in the freight elevator, grateful for her bravery and dedication to the fight. What was a simple Prueba had turned into something more significant. Through Hil's guidance, the young woman had grown remarkably in just a few days. Esperanza, as Hil's witness, took pride in having played a role in her development and a small smile graced her lips.

Lyric and Jalin positioned themselves in the small elevator, with Jalin taking the lead on the rope. The device was not designed for transporting people, but the two squeezed into the cramped space. Esperanza watched cautiously as her counterpart pulled the rope to start the ascent. Lyric and Jalin disappeared from her view and ascended into the ceiling. The slow but steady sounds of gears and pulleys, combined with the rumble of thunder outside, caused a commotion among the storage room's occupants. The horses seemed particularly agitated. Esperanza knew they couldn't afford to lose their only means of escape. She forced herself to stand and walked to the mouth of the tunnel.

As she turned to face the darkness, an eerie silence enveloped the room. The eyes of the caged occupants were fixed on her, their attention was focused beyond her. She slowly turned her head, to see the outline of a figure standing in the tunnel's shadows.

She wasn't alone.

The figure remained motionless, hands open and reaching into the light of the room. Their skin bore a hauntingly inhuman pallor, and their nails were dirty but menacingly sharp.

Taking a sharp breath, Esperanza prepared herself for what would come.

"Please Voca," a rough voice said, "I need your help… "

DARK TIDES

Lightning flashed from beyond the closed doors of the tiny freight elevator. Crammed together in its tight space, Lyric and Jalin waited for the car to come to a full stop. Gears clanked and wood groaned under their weight.

Jalin pressed his ear against the small opening of the doors and listened for movement. He gestured with his chin at Lyric.

"Ready your pistols," he whispered.

She nodded and withdrew them, then waited for his signal.

Thunder cracked, following the lightning. The storm had arrived.

Jalin carefully pushed one door open and peered into a small pantry. Content that it was clear, he pushed the other door open. They carefully climbed out of the elevator.

The room appeared untouched. Lyric noted dishes and leftover foodstuffs on the counters. Her brow furrowed. She hissed softly at Jalin and nodded at them.

"Those are left from when we were here."

He scowled. "You are certain?"

Lyric looked closer at the items and nodded.

Lightning flashed once more, briefly illuminating the pantry area from the tiny ventilation windows by the ceiling. The door from the pantry to the dining hall was closed. Cool air rushed in from beneath the door, sending crumbs and dust scuttling across the floor.

Why was the wind blowing through the dining hall?

Jalin approached the door and placed his hand on its flat surface and then listened once more. He held up three fingers, then slowly counted down to one and pushed the door open.

Destruction and disarray.

Shattered glass littered the floor and covered the furniture. The giant stained glass windows had blown in, the wind gusting through their gutted and open remains as the storm's fury howled outside. Broken chairs and overturned tables lay before them.

Jalin surveyed the area quickly.

He pointed at several areas on the floor with noticeable scuff marks from boots. One wall bore a body-shaped indentation in its white plastered surface.

"There was a fight here," he said.

"Carson?" Lyric asked.

Jalin pursed his lips. "Perhaps." He checked the edge of his scoring blade.

The doors at the far end of the dining hall hung precariously on their hinges. One door swung loose, slamming into the wall as the wind pushed it open.

Giving Lyric a nod, he advanced to the door and into the open courtyard.

Rain poured down from the darkened sky above. Jalin and Lyric flattened themselves against the wall of the building and slowly skirted the edge of the courtyard. A silvery glow caught Lyric's eye. The El-EmGee sat in its cradle as the rain washed down over it, adding to the small stream in the center of the courtyard. Its light was comforting. Part of her yearned to walk into the rain, to the small island where it sat, curl up there, and just wait everything out.

A spine-chilling scream filled the air and shattered her wandering thoughts.

"That came from inside the Shrine," Jalin said. He cautiously headed toward the sound.

Lyric gave the El-EmGee one final glance and followed reluctantly behind him.

As they made their way toward the Shrine, they passed a pair of doors. Jalin paused. One door had been broken open. Its splintered remains lay scattered on the ground. An odd smell lingered in the air.

"Something broke into the Armory," Jalin said quietly and looked into the room.

Lyric peeked under his arm and into the room beyond. A shape reminiscent of an armor rack sat in the back corner with a sheet draped over it. The room appeared neat and orderly.

"Is anything missing?" she asked.

Jalin's eyes scoured the room and came to rest on a sword rack on the far wall.

"Short sword and a dueling dagger," he responded. His eyes lingered on the armor rack for a moment, then he turned away. "Let's move," he said and led them down the hall.

The unholy howls grew louder. Wood groaned. Glass shattered. It was the sound of vampyres shrieking in the night.

The pair moved down the hall toward the Shrine Marshall's quarters. The rooms that Gale Stonebridge should have occupied. A soft light emanated from under the closed door. From across the way, the sounds of vampyres battling someone continued. Jalin quickly moved to the Marshall's door and pushed it open carefully.

A small, simple bedroom equipped with a bed, dressing stand and a desk lay beyond. In the center of the room sat Stonebridge's Mechanist Chair. The worn red blanket the Judex wore across his knees lay on the ground. The Judex was not present. Nor were there signs of violence. The bed was neatly made and did not appear slept in.

Jalin bent to scoop up the threadbare blanket. He pressed it to his nose for a moment and inhaled deeply.

His eyes hardened. He tossed the piece of fabric to the side. It floated down and lay on the bed.

Discarded and forgotten.

"Come on," Jalin said and strode toward the Shrine's waiting doors.

The once peaceful and welcoming shrine was now a haunting stage set for the dark tides of destruction.

Splintered benches lay in ruins, scattered about like forgotten relics of better times. The storm outside mirrored the turmoil within, as if the forces of nature themselves sensed the malevolence emanating from the room. Raindrops merged with spilled blood, painting the floor in macabre hues.

Amidst the tempestuous backdrop, two sinister figures engaged in a deadly dance around a third. Their movements were almost hypnotic. Vampyric hisses echoed like ominous whispers all around them. Long, jagged cuts adorned the vampyres' bodies, inflicted in a battle that would have claimed the lives of mortals.

In the center of the room stood the target of their fury: Gale Stonebridge. His right hand brandished a short sword and his left held a dagger at the ready. Both were covered in blood and ichor. He moved with youthful vigor and skill. A true exemplar of his calling. Power and prowess emanated from his physique.

This could not be the same man she met two days prior. That man was confined to the Life Support Chair in the other room. Were her suspicions correct? Had a doppelgänger taken the place of a Judex, as they had Queen Marisol?

Lyric's eyes slid over to Jalin. He stood motionless, his eyes fixated on the scene before him.

Movement. Gale's stance shifted. His arms opened wide in a taunting invitation. There was an air of cockiness about him, born from years of facing the most terrifying horrors this world offered. As if responding to an unseen summons, both creatures lunged forward with terrifying speed. Their movements defied nature, each step covering impossible distances as their clawed hands sliced through the air.

Gale matched them, step for step. Claws were blocked with blades. Teeth were blocked with metal vambraces. Every swing and parry was a blur of motion. The clash of steel and claw resonated like the thunder overhead, shaking the chamber with a sinister reverberation.

An opening.

A step to the side.

Striking claws were dodged as the blade of Gale's sword drew across the chest of one creature. He spun on his heel and brought the blade up to meet the second vampyre. It was all fast. Impossibly fast.

Lyric watched his body move, realizing his speed was beyond human and completely unnatural. A sinking feeling filled her chest.

For a split second, it appeared as though Gale's attack on the second vampyre missed. But the creature hung in mid-step for a moment, eyes wide, fanged mouth agape. Its body convulsed and split in two, collapsing dead on the floor.

Behind Gale, the other vampyre bellowed in rage.

Gale spun to face his opponent. He opened his mouth and emitted an equally unholy howl of fury and challenge. His eyes were bottomless pools of black ink. His mouth filled with impossibly sharp teeth.

This was not a doppelgänger.

This was Gale Stonebridge, and he was a vampyre.

"NOOOOOOOOOO!" Jalin screamed. Tears streamed from the Inquisitor's wrath-filled eyes, "HOW COULD YOU!"

Stonebridge jerked his head toward the Inquisitor's cry. He balked. The monstrous mask disappeared from view, replaced once more by the humble man. His eyes fixated on Jalin standing in the doorway. An expression of shame colored his expression.

"My son... "

Quick to seize upon the distraction, the vampyre lept in and clawed Gale's back, slashing through his clothing and rending flesh. It darted quickly toward a far door and out of the Shrine. Gale howled in pain. The temporary facade of humanity was ripped away in the moment and replaced once more by the monster.

"You stupid child!" Gale snarled at Jalin. "You're letting it get away!" Wasting no time, Gale chased after the creature as it disappeared out of sight.

Swallowing a strangled sob of anger and betrayal, an enraged Jalin shoved past Lyric to give chase.

Off balance, she was flung toward an alcove. Narrowly catching herself, her pistol flew from her hand and spun across the stone floor, and came to rest against a pile of broken benches. She braced herself on the alcove's edge for a moment, trying to catch her breath.

The pile of broken wood shifted and from within its depths, a figure emerged. Covered in blood and gore, a lone vampyre crawled out of the debris. A large wooden chair leg emerged from the center of its chest. With clawed hands, it dragged the wood free of its body. It let out a pained hiss and tossed the makeshift weapon aside.

Lyric eyed the pistol on the ground at the base of the pile of furniture. With a shaky hand, she drew her remaining weapon and pointed the muzzle at the vampyre.

Hil protect me...

The creature eyed her suspiciously and drew its lips in a manner not unlike a scowl. Its eyes examined her carefully. These were not the eyes of an irrational beast. There was intelligence here.

It spoke.

"Not... here... for you," it said.

Lyric kept her pistol trained on the creature as it limped toward the doorway and pushed through the door.

"They're intelligent... oh gods, what is happening?" she said aloud. Shots rang out in the distance.

"Jalin!" Picking up the dropped pistol, she rushed out the door.

THE HAND OF FAITH

C louds obscured the night sky and rain continued to fall as the combatants converged in the courtyard.

By the time Lyric rounded the corner, the battle was nearly over. Decades of training combined with supernatural strength and speed gave Gale the upper hand. At his feet lay a vampyre, arms and legs haphazardly twisted and bent. Blood oozed from its injuries, blended with the rainwater, and seeped into the ground. The Judex stood, arm outstretched with impossibly strong fingers wrapped like iron around the throat of the second monster. He held it aloft with no more effort than a child's broken toy. The creature hissed and clawed pointlessly at Gale's hand, feet kicking wildly in the air.

Opposite him stood Jalin. Scoring blade readied, he pointed the muzzle of his pistol at the Judex.

"This?" the creature wearing the face of the Judex spat as it glared at the vampyre in his grip. "No. This is not my work. I did not create this... thing."

The creature's words echoed in Lyric's mind. *Not here for you...*

They were here for Gale!

But why?

"Creator or no, you are one of them," Jalin replied. "A monster, killing monsters."

Gale laughed at the words. It was a dark sound. Lyric shivered to hear it.

"No boy. I am a survivor."

"At what cost?!" Jalin countered. "Look at what you have become!"

The creature squirmed in Gale's grip. Panicked eyes searched the courtyard and finally found Lyric.

"Help... me..." it pleaded.

Lyric gasped, her hand quickly raising to cover her mouth. Jalin cocked his pistol.

A look of shock flooded Gale's features as the creature spoke. It was quickly replaced with disgust.

"You will find no mercy from me, monster... " Gale whispered to the vampyre. He squeezed tightly into the creature's throat. It convulsed in a frantic attempt to escape. With an audible POP, the convulsions became light spasms, and then the creature went limp.

Gale dropped the body to the ground. It collapsed in a lifeless heap. He looked at Jalin, who still had his pistol pointed in his direction.

"Still not satisfied?" Gale asked. With a disgusted snarl, he raised his booted foot and swiftly brought the heel down on the creature's skull. It collapsed in a terrible sound beneath the force of the blow. Raising his foot, he scowled at the mess and scuffed his heel against the wet pavement to wipe away the remains. He turned his gaze once more on Jalin.

"I say again... I did not create these abominations."

"No?" Jalin asked. "Then tell me, *Father*." The word dripped with pain and venom. "Who made you? How are you like this now?"

Gale paused. "Will you listen if I tell you?"

Jalin's aim wavered. He lowered the muzzle of the weapon. "Go on."

Gale inclined his head in what appeared to be polite thanks and stepped out of the rain and under an overhang. Jalin followed suit, maintaining his distance. The silver etchings on his scoring blade glowed brightly in the darkness.

Gale smiled softly and sheathed his weapons. He raised his right hand and slowly traced a line down the middle of his chest. "Do you know what it is like to have a machine breathe for you?" The question was riddled with pain. "Carasin is an unforgiving death. I had tubes for air and a pump that replaced my heart. More tubes to cleanse my blood and return it to my body."

Jalin's expression softened. Concern replaced anger.

"The Vocas did their duty. They told me to make my peace. To take care of all the things that dying men needed to take care of." Gale looked over at Jalin. "So the living could go on when I was gone."

Jalin's eyes twitched. A moment of sorrow touched his dark gaze.

Gale growled suddenly and spat, "Witches! I hated them! Hil's light is eternal! Hil's voice is life!" He flung his arm wide, gesturing back toward the Shrine. "They could heal my wounds!" He turned back to face Jalin. His expression was filled with anger. "You have seen their... miracles. All they had to do was... ask the right question... utter the right prayer."

Jalin's brow furrowed.

"They said what I asked was unholy. Forbidden. They refused. Refused ME. The greatest warrior of its Order. Its most dutiful soldier. Its Hand of Faith." He pulled his sword from its sheath then and stepped forward. With a roar of anger, he drove its blade into the corpse of the vampyre there.

"They denied me their gifts! The Voice of Hil denied me the ability to live, to fight, to breathe. To be a man!" Gale stood tall and turned his face toward the heavens. The rain fell onto his upturned face and washed away the blood and battle. If the Judex shed tears, it was unknown, but the raw emotion was real.

Jalin's stance wavered. Lyric's eyes darted to the Inquisitor. Red stains trailed down his back and abdomen from wounds previously obscured by the rain. Whether from the claws of vampyres or stab wounds from Gale's dagger, she could not tell. Jalin's jaw clenched tight as he forced himself to remain standing.

To perform his duty.

Gale moved slowly around Jalin. "No celebration of honors achieved. No memorial. No accolades. Nothing. They sent me here to quietly die. Alone. Years of knowledge... years of experience... all gone! All because of one stupid mistake! Such a stupid mistake that even you would have made."

Gale's eyes searched the courtyard.

He's looking for me and Esperanza! Lyric thought. She ducked into the shadows and out of sight.

Gale continued to maneuver around Jalin. Each step forced the Inquisitor to adjust, to shift, to pivot painfully in order to keep his eyes on the Judex.

"It doesn't matter who provided me with this opportunity. What matters is I seized control of my story. This is not corruption or heresy. No. This is taking the weapons and tools of darkness and turning them for OUR use!"

Gale stood before Jalin, staring down at the younger man. "Look at me, son," he said. "This gift saved my life." Gale's eyes were no longer hungry black pools, but the bright blue eyes of an earnest father. He slowly extended his hand to Jalin.

"Come with me, son. Join me. Stand with me in this, so we can carry on the Glory of Hil. I cannot trust anyone else with this. You are the only one I can depend on. The only one I need at my side."

Jalin stared at the outstretched hand. His anger and frustration faded. His head dropped slightly and his shoulders slumped. His pistol fell to the ground. The gentle rain fell heavier as Jalin looked back at his father's hand. The arm bearing the scoring blade hung limply at Jalin's side. He pressed the other against his stomach, the blood slowly seeping between his fingers. The fight in his eyes faded to nothing.

No, no, no, no, no! Lyric screamed in her head. She could not let it end like this. Not like this! Taking a deep breath, she drew the silvered blade that Jalin gave her and ran toward Gale.

"Come now, Jalin," Gale said reassuringly. "Come with me and I will show you the way."

Gale screamed suddenly as the silvered blade slid into his back. His face twisted into a monstrous visage once more. Rows of sharpened teeth snarled into the night air as dark, inhuman eyes searched wildly around. The sound of sizzling flesh hissed as the blade sank further. Gale flailed wildly, trying to reach the source of the pain. Successful in her attack, Lyric tried to dodge Gale's angry grasp but was not quick enough. Gale turned and snatched the young scribe by her hair. Lifting her off the ground, he twisted and pulled the blade out of his back. It clattered to the ground.

"Women," he spat, "They are the weakness of humanity." With casual effort, he tossed Lyric across the courtyard like a rag doll. Her limp form slammed into the base that held the El-Em Gee.

Gale whirled back to face Jalin. "Look at me, my son. Look at me!" Gale implored.

Before Jalin could answer, a shadowy figure lept from the rooftop and slammed into Gale, sending him into the stone floor. Soaked by the rain, the unkempt figure crawled atop the prone Judex and pounded his head into the stone floor.

Across the courtyard, Lyric struggled into a seated position. She used the obelisk that cradled the El EmGee to support her. Rainwater ran over the obelisk, across the glowing stone, and washed over her injured body. Her pain lessened. She tried to focus on the activity before her.

Two figures scrambled and fought in the mud and rain of the courtyard. One was the figure of Gale Stonebridge. The other appeared to be a disheveled-looking woman. The speed and ferocity of the woman made it clear to Lyric that these were both vampyres.

Kneeling apart from the battling figures, was Jalin Cortez. The injured Inquisitor's legs had finally betrayed his will to stand.

Focus, Lyric. Stay Focused.

The water from the El-EmGee continued to wash over her broken body. It was cool and refreshing.

In the courtyard, the two vampyres tried to kill each other.

Despite the savagery of the woman's attack, Gale was quick to recover. He slammed his fist into the woman's chest, sending her sprawling back. Standing, he stared down at her with disdain in his eyes, which soon changed to recognition.

"You!"

The woman hissed at him in response and rolled into a standing position. "How nice of you to finally remember what you left behind, Judex."

Gale snarled at her and jerked his sword out of the ground. "All of this destruction is yours?" He pointed the blade at her.

The woman stood slowly, "A fair price for your sins."

"Explain yourself, creature!" Gale demanded.

"You don't deserve an explanation!" she growled and launched herself at him once more.

He stepped to the side and ducked. The woman flew past him, claws that would have raked across his chest ripping across his face instead. He howled in pain and twisted. She landed beyond him, tucking and rolling into a ready position.

"You left me for dead, but I didn't die. I DIDN'T DIE!" she yelled at him. "Death would have been a mercy." She scrambled quickly away.

Gale snarled and strode to pursue the woman. "An accident created in the infancy of my condition. You were a mistake... One I intend to correct!"

In a sudden burst of quickened ferocity, the woman leaped at Gale, catching him off guard despite his years of rigorous training. She seized the opportunity, her sharpened nails leaving a deep gash across Gale's throat as they drew additional droplets of crimson blood. He howled in pain and brought an iron fist up, connecting with her stomach. She flew upward, catching her shoulder on the edge of the roof tiles. She shrieked in response.

"You killed my son! My husband!" she yelled at Gale."They ATE MY FATHER!" She screamed at Gale. He swung the sword at her. She darted out of the range of the weapon's edge.

"And how many died to slake *your* hunger?" Gale demanded.

A look of shame covered the woman's face for a moment. "I did what was necessary. I am not proud of it. Are you?"

She shifted her position and circled Gale. He watched her carefully, keeping the sword pointed at her. "The more I fed, the more I remembered. I remembered who I was, and I remembered you." She motioned to the bodies on the ground. "All of this was because of you. I survived so I can take everything you took from me." She looked at Jalin. "Your legacy... Your name... " She smiled with razored teeth. "Yes, I know your name, Gale Stonebridge, Judex of the First. I am Dolores Gouveia, and I am here for vengeance." She smiled and launched herself at Gale. Ferocity and revenge powered her savage blows.

Pain surged through Gale, his training and muscle memory taking over. He rolled back with uncanny grace, evading Dolores's oncoming strikes with an unnatural fluidity.

With a swift, arching motion, Gale unleashed a powerful boot on Dolores's jaw. She reeled in agony. Righting himself, he cast his sword aside. Charging forward like a wrathful specter, Gale closed the distance with unyielding determination.

Dolores struggled to recover from the force of the kick, but it was too late. Gale was upon her. He seized one of her legs and effortlessly hoisted her into the air. With merciless resolve, he slammed her body against the unforgiving stone surface. A chilling mixture of anguish and rage filled the air as Gale continued his relentless assault. The sickening crack of bones echoed across the courtyard. The surface of the pale stones was stained the dark crimson of spilled blood.

Gale stood over Dolores' broken body and placed his boot on her neck. He sneered down at her. Dolores opened her mouth to force out a single cry, but only a fat bubble of blood popped out and ran down her face.

Gale smiled at the woman. "Commendable. A multi-pronged attack, hitting the Shrine during the day, as well as the night. A bit amateurish, but still commendable." Seeing no fight from the woman, he stepped off of her.

"You were not soldiers," the Judex said. He reached down and wrapped his hand around her throat, and pulled her off the ground. "A Shrine in the mountains would have stopped the ghouls. That is on your people." He stared into her face. "In the beginning, the hunger is ceaseless. It was an unconscious action, a simple mistake. That is all you are. A mistake. I am not your father, nor your creator, or your progenitor. I am merely a dutiful soldier cleaning up a mistake. If it means so much to you, Ms. Gouveia, I apologize."

From the muddy ground, Jalin moved. He shifted and brought the silvered scoring blade up defiantly.

Gale glanced over at the Inquisitor and sighed. He tossed Dolores to the side and calmly walked over to Jalin's bleeding form.

"Following the faith of Hil and the will of the Order is what everyone must do if they want to survive the night. I would have you at my side, my son. But I cannot leave you to stand against me."

"At the cost of his soul?!" Lyric's voice called out.

Gale narrowed his eyes and turned. The young Scribe still sat against the obelisk.

"Look around you!" she said. "Look at what this place has become under your care! Is this the legacy of the Great Gale Stonebridge, Judex of the First?"

"You dare speak of legacy…" Gale stalked toward Lyric. "You do not understand what legacy is. You don't even bear the mark of adulthood."

"And yet it will be me… or someone like me… who records your name for history."

Gale's lips curled up into a sneer. He reached out to grab her once again. An invisible wall of pain and power stopped him. His hands sizzled. Wincing, Gale jerked his hand away from Lyric. His flesh blistered. He stared at the wound, and then back at the woman with water running over her head and across her now uninjured body. The glow from the El-EmGee saturated the water as it passed across its strange surface.

Gale's eyes widened. "It has other uses…"

Gale's eyes continued to widen and his mouth opened in a scream of unholy torment as the tip of a silvered blade burst through his chest from behind. Screaming in agony, he grasped at the tip of the blade. His hands sizzled against the silver. Lyric watched in horror as she realized the truth - the blade had pierced Gale's heart, a wound from which even his newfound immortality could not save him. Looking past him, she saw Jalin holding the blade, his eyes filled with cool rage. He twisted the blade then, as the sound of burning skin mixed with Gale's screams. He pulled the silvered instrument free. Gale collapsed to the ground, his body trembling with pain as his lifeblood stained the ground beneath him.

Looking up, he locked eyes with Jalin. "... why?"

Jalin looked down at the creature who had once been Gale Stonebridge. "... because this is what my father taught me." With a swift strike, Jalin brought his scoring blade across Gale's neck, releasing his head from his shoulders.

Overhead, the rain finally ceased.

Lyric quickly pushed herself up to stand and stepped across the small water barrier and the safety of the El-EmGee.

"Cortez... " she reached out to him and he fell into her arms as his strength finally left him. She looked down into his face. He was pale and worn. Blood continued to seep from his wounds. "What has he done to you?"

A slow growl emanated from behind them. The Scribe and the Inquisitor looked back to see Dolores, battered and broken, but standing. She loomed over the corpse of the Judex.

Jalin tried to lift his arm to bring the scoring blade between the vampyre and them.

"Peace, Inquisition. Peace." Dolores whispered. Above them, the storm clouds parted, and the stars peered down from the heavens.

She turned tired eyes on the pair. "We who live beyond the walls struggle to find our place in this world. Do not squander yours." She reached into her pocket and pulled out a tiny silver vial. It sizzled in her hand.

Lyric looked around the courtyard, searching for Esperanza.

"Where... did you get that?" Jalin asked.

Dolores gave somewhat of a bitter smile. "The Voca... She has done a great service by gifting me this." She stared at the vial and then at the pair on the ground. "She is fine, but you should go to her now."

Lyric began pulling Jalin to his feet.

Dolores looked down at the body of Gale. "We should not be. We should not be like this," she said and slowly opened the small capsule. She looked at Lyric and Jalin and released the red fluid over her head.

"Run."

Pulling on the last of their reserves, Lyric limped Jalin out of the courtyard as the air around them burst into flames.

THE VOLVER

A cavalcade of color decorated the normally conservative streets of the Imperial Capitol. Cutouts of hawks, suns, and shields interlinked on banners of green, white, and gold spanning every street and every corner. The symbols and colors of the Imperial family. Smaller banners hung from lampposts and awnings. The Capitol was festive and welcoming.

The early afternoon light illuminated the silver hawk of the Imperium as it soared across its lush green field. All along the street, people laughed, drank, and ate. Small groups of musicians wandered and played their guitars, violins, and horns.

The week-long celebration of Verdad was coming to a close. Its culmination, the Volver, would be held today.

Lyric leaned out the window of her apartments and gazed down into the square below. It was filled with attendants and families. In the main City Square, they would be preparing for the investitures and appointments of office and station.

In the distance, the rhythmic sounds of bells ringing told her she had an hour left. The formal ceremony would start at noon and after that be the final celebration.

She made it.

Her eyes searched the crowd below. *So many people!*

In the times before the Corpse Wars, the Verdad was a simple coming-of-age ceremony. It was celebrated in every village and town with music and cakes and dancing. After the War, Verdad took on a deeper meaning within the newly formed Imperium. Now it stood as a testament of allegiance and support for every member of the Imperium. To undergo Verdad showed a willingness to accept the responsibility of being part of the Imperium. It was to accept one's place in the world and become a Servant of the Throne.

As youth approached an age of reason and decision-making, they were encouraged to choose their professions and apprentice within those ranks. They would eventually undergo Verdad and Prueba. Their time of challenge and quest for truth. All would venture beyond the Imperial Cities. Some would choose simple tasks that may take them no further than a Guild Waystation for a week. Others would choose journeys that would take them much further away from their homes.

The Verdad was a statement of intent from a child.

The Volver heralded the return of an adult.

In Imperium understood the importance of such an act. This was not merely signing one's name to a document. This was potentially taking up arms against the horrors beyond the Walls and risking one's life.

The Verdad was honored.

The Volver was celebrated.

As the Harvest Season approached, the Otoñal was welcomed and the banners of Volver were hung. Those who had completed their Verdad earlier in the year would be welcomed just as warmly as those who arrived the day before. All were welcome. All were celebrated.

No expense was spared for the week of the Volver. No family was turned away. Imperial coffers paid every expense for the celebrants. New clothes and uniforms were provided. New weapons and gear assigned. All in thanks and exchange for an Oath of Service to the Throne.

Lyric sighed deeply. She gingerly touched the newly inked tattoo that marked her Oath of Service. Her red quill. Deirdre had stood with Lyric as it was applied. The ink was only a few days old, and she felt an underlying itch wanting to emerge. The pain of the tattoo had been minimal compared to the ordeal of the week prior.

The Librarian had not left her side once Lyric returned. They had received two missives from the Great Gates, but it had been the one that carried the Voca's sigil which spurred action.

"I am so proud of you!" the older woman said as she pulled Lyric into her arms and pressed her lips to her forehead.

There had been conversation and questions then. She remembered turning all of her journals over to Dierdre, who took them away for transcription and promised they would be returned.

Lyric turned away from the window and sought the full-length mirror in the room. It was a beautiful gown in green and gold, the colors of her office. The skirts were full, and the waist was narrow. Her red hair cascaded down her back in ringlet curls across her ivory shoulders and was adorned with roses of brilliant gold.

Most of her injuries had healed, thanks to the care of the Vocas and the magic of the El-EmGee. A pink scar on her throat was the only visible trophy of her ordeal. Her fingers traced the lines where creatures born of legend had tried to kill her.

"A display for another time." She told herself and reached for a green and gold choker. She carefully clasped it around her neck and adjusted it to hide the wound.

A soft knock interrupted her musing.

Her heart leaped a moment. She took a breath and stepped to the door, carefully pulling it open.

An older man stood on the other side of the doorway. His white hair and beard were neatly trimmed. He wore the black and gold of the Order.

"Scribe Wax?" he asked. "I am Escritora Tomas. May I come in?"

Lyric frowned a little but drew the door open. "Of course. How may I be of service?"

Tomas smiled as he entered the room. His brilliant blue eyes quickly surveyed the area and then returned to her.

"thank you for your efforts to record the events of Paraíso Verde. They have been reviewed and will be cataloged as necessary."

"Thank you? I was simply doing my duty… "

"And it is appreciated." He held out his hand to her. She accepted it. His hands were warm and gentle. "We understand that you have experienced great trauma and witnessed a tremendous event. We want you to know that we understand the rigors that you withstood, and appreciate your sacrifices."

Lyric's brow furrowed. "I don't understand?"

Tomas' eyes were kind and full of compassion. "I am certain you understand that the events of Paraíso Verde are still under investigation… and it is important to control the narrative of what happened."

"Control the… you want me to lie?" she said flatly.

"Not at all," Tomas countered. "You showed exceptional care in how you recorded the events of Paraíso Verde and exercised solid judgment in the information you shared with both Gallegos and Hudson. You are to be commended."

"Then what do you need from me?"

Tomas smiled, "Simply your patience while we finish our investigations. The matter of Judex Stonebridge is… delicate, and we need to prevent panic while we ascertain how he came into his… hmmm… condition."

"I… understand." She replied.

"We knew you would." He smiled once more and gently squeezed her hand. "We could use a woman of your talents, Ms. Wax."

Lyric flinched slightly and pulled her hand away from Tomas' grasp.

"You would still be a Servant of the Throne, mind you... but the Order has a need for talented individuals, such as yourself. You would be an Escritora... a field writer. You would accompany our people into the field and give validity to their stories."

"A... Historian?"

Tomas shrugged a little. "Of a sort, yes. Consider it? We'd love to have you aboard."

Lyric took a breath and tugged at the edges of her corset.

"You'll have my answer before the night is done."

She may not have been the tallest one at the ceremony, but she was the oldest. Many of those being celebrated were in their mid-teens, all young adults. Several celebrants and a few parents cast disparaging looks at Lyric as she stood among them. She knew it was uncommon for someone to wait as long as she had to undergo her trials. Tonight she was an adult and old enough to enjoy a glass of wine while her fellows were relegated to punch. She toasted them with all sincerity. They, like she, had made it.

Representatives from all the Orders and Guilds, as well as clergy from the Temples of each deity, the University Scholars, and the Fugue Academy, were all present. It was the single time of year when each might be seen in the company of the others without the threat of harm.

The Trinity of Hil, Geekind, and Styx gave their blessings on the celebrants, their families, and the Imperium, wishing them each prosperity for the upcoming year. Each then stepped aside to welcome initiates into their ranks and adorn them with their robes of service. The Clergy of Hil in golds, the Followers of Geekind in browns and greens, and the Servants of Styx in black.

Lyric's eyes followed a black-robed figure bearing the sigils of Styx, the God of the Dead.

"Better today than tomorrow," Lyric said to herself as she sipped her wine and watched the group. Tomorrow would be the Pena, the Day of Sorrow. The observation for those who did not return. It was one of the few days of the year when the sigils of Styx would be on open display. The Order of Hil kept a wary eye on the Servants of the God of the Dead, but even they understood the role of Styx in ensuring the departed did not haunt the living.

"Are these seats taken?"

Looking up, Lyric saw Esperanza standing there in her formal attire. The simple yellow and white cotton robes she had become accustomed to seeing her in had been replaced with formal robes of gold and ivory. Elegantly embroidered sigils followed along the cuffs and hem of both. Her dark hair was plaited and draped over her right shoulder. Her face was full and healthy like the first day they had met.

Lyric bolted from her chair, jostling the table with her full skirts. "Esperanza!" She shifted to hold open her arms. "I have missed you!"

Esperanza pulled the younger woman into a welcome and warm embrace. "We are very proud of you, Lyric."

"Thank you… wait, we?" Lyric asked.

Releasing the embrace, Esperanza nodded toward a lone figure leaning against a wall. "He's over there… being himself."

Looking over, Lyric saw Jalin Cortez eyeing them both. No blades, no armor, wearing only a simple black charro suit with a white shirt and green ribbon tie.

Lyric leaned over to Esperanza and whispered, "I know he's not here unarmed. How many weapons do you think he snuck in?"

"At least two knives in his boots, and probably a single-shot pistol in his jacket," the Voca replied softly and smiled politely at the Manos.

He raised his glass at the both of them. Suddenly, his eyes narrowed.

"Am I allowed to congratulate my patient, sister?" said a voice from behind them.

The voice was familiar. Lyric remembered it briefly from their travel back from the Shrine. There had been a group from The Order sent to meet them. Summoned by Esperanza's sigil. The voice belonged to the woman that traveled with them. A healer.

"You are welcome to speak with Cortez, Lupe, but I don't know how happy he will be to see you," Esperanza replied.

Lyric turned to find the owner of the familiar voice. A woman dressed in the yellows and ivories of Hil stood before her. Unlike the conservative Esperanza, the sigils on the new woman's robes were in black silk, and her neckline exposed both shoulders. Peeking out of the collar and along her shoulders were elaborate designs of holy sigils, married with vine work and flowers. Her hair was woven into a complex braided crown. Fresh roses were neatly tucked in the knots.

These were not what set the woman apart from Esperanza. It was her face. The entire left side of her face was tattooed in an intricate skull mask. White and gold makeup accented the dark lines. She was striking.

"Oh, not him. I meant this wonderful flower!" the woman said. She wiggled her fingers at Jalin. He glowered in return.

Esperanza shook her head, "Lyric Wax, may I present Voca Guadalupe Teresa Casteneda. She is the one who ensured we did not die on the way home," Esperanza said. "And yes, Lupe, you can say hello to your patient." turning back to Lyric, she continued. "I will keep our friend company," she said, indicating Jalin, and walked over to join him. He continued to glower in Lupe's direction.

"He's a sour one, isn't he?" she said as he took a seat next to Lyric. "Tell me, how are you feeling? No more dizzy spells or headaches?"

Lyric sat next to her. "Not as much. Haven't had a dizzy spell for the last few days," she paused, "So you weren't a dream?"

"Well, it depends on who you ask..." Lupe said with a bit mischievousness, "If you ask Senor Frowny Face over there, I am probably a nightmare. But no, it was not a dream. I was with the group that found the three of you outside of the shrine. I did enough to give you a fighting chance. The rest was up to you and Hil's mercy. That one," she motioned to Jalin, "was nearly dead, and refused treatment. If Esperanza hadn't been there to talk some sense into him... that man!" She rolled her eyes to the heavens. "Hil grant us patience for Jalin Cortez! He demanded I help you first. De-man-ded. Whether he says it or not, he cares about you. Be careful with his kind though..."

"His kind?" Lyric asked.

"Manos are a tough breed, but not always long for this world. Don't give too much of your heart, little flower, or you may lose it entirely when they are gone. At least that is what my father taught me," Lupe said.

Lyric blushed slightly and started to speak, but Lupe hushed her, " Hush now. I have three gifts for you, Lyric Wax. One," she said, and as she pulled a silver ring off of her finger and slid it on Lyric's finger right pinky. "That is a gift from me to you because you pulled through." Taking her right hand, she gently kissed the back of Lyric's hand. "That is a blessing for your health and the life to come. Live and love the life you have been given. And always remember... even in the darkness, there are those that care for you."

Nodding, Lyric smiled, "Thank you."

"And the third is this Escorita. Give this to your Manos, he will need to see it," Lupe said as she handed her an envelope with a seal of the Order.

"But... I haven't chosen," Lyric said in slight protest.

"Of course you have, mi mariposa," Lupe said as she stood. "This life has marked you. You just need to accept it. I will see you on the dance floor later, right?"

Standing, Lyric reached out and hugged Lupe, "Thank you,"

"Live and love, that is how you thank me," she said and then wandered away.

Walking over to her companions, she held out the envelope to Jalin. "This is for you."

Esperanza raised an eyebrow, recognizing the envelope. "I take it you have decided?"

Lyric nodded. "I will need to talk to Deidra... but yes, I have."

Esperanza smiled and then looked at Jalin. "New orders?"

Jalin frowned. "It's a recall mission. They want someone picked up and transported to the Fugue Academy." He handed it back to Lyric. "Find out what you can about them so we can prepare."

Esperanza asked, "If they are to go to the Fugue Academy, are we dealing with a mage? Who are we after?"

Lyric read the letter and shook her head. "I have no idea. Have you ever heard of Emilio Kane?"

~The End~

RECORD MANAGEMENT

ARTICLE 12 - SECTION 1A

It must be SANCTIONED by a Grain Officer

Mints as decreed by the Imperium or Imperium reprentatives, and associated guilds will require a detailed accounting and record of any and all associated documents concerning a homestead's day to day expenditures as well timely reports of certain commodity products such as, but not limted to wheat, grains, corn, etc.

Planning and Land Management

Farming for profit (based on current Imperium rates) verses a family-centric operation (see Article 15 for rules of operation on a family-centric business) still bear an equal amount of work and scrutiny on both the land health and seasonal weather conditions. While the Imperium encourages a family model - we are more than happy to support any attempts at a regular business farm. However, in doing so, adhereance to the overall Codex Deber in full will be required. Good record-keeping helps the family and Imperium on track for a successful year, outside of any environmental disaster or mishap (see Article 86 for a full listing of accpeted natural disasters). Also it is up to the individual to keep track of season price changes as they should be reflected in logs.

Profit and Maintenance

Grain Officers are entrusted with the authority of the Imperium to review, and scrutinize all record keeping to insure accurate records if the farm in question choose to work as a profit venture. If the reviewed records do not match or if the accounting is off, the Grain Officer will have the authorition to oversee a full inspection as well as an

HISLOP'S GUIDE TO THE NATURAL WORLD

VOLUME 6 - EXOTIC FAUNA

EXERPT BY BEX GRELL, DVM

SANCTIONED BY
THE GRAND ARCHIVE

IMPERIUM OF KRAPHAX

CANIS ARANEAE (CONT)

MOVEMENT (CONTINUED)

...comparison to other large mammals, there are some similarities to the great cats of the feline family. Upon examination of their paws, they possess the same type of skin exposure and gripping capabilities as both species. However, the current theory for their ability to remain silent is because of the sound dampening qualities of their coat. Based on what limited observation in the wild that can be had, it may be a combination of both the fur element, additional limbs, and joint control similar to the arachnid family.

Further study on additional limbs and their natural augmentation has many wondering whether the Daerrog is truly a naturally occurring creature or if it results from experimentation of species cross-breeding.

Field Sketch by B. Wolfram, Peackeeper

Whether by chance or design, the additional limbs serve the creature well for running silently at its top speed (recorded at 74 km per hour as of publication), though it is uncer...

Acknowledgements

There are a lot of hands (and minds) that help a project cross the finish line. We would like to thank some of the folx that helped make this journey possible:

To our spouses: Julie & Kirk – thank you for putting up with weekly meetings, late-night phone calls, and odd one-way conversations that may have sounded like we were off our rockers. Thank you also for sitting with us at book signings and schlepping gear all over the place. This is a partnership, and we could not do this without you.

To Finley: Dude! Seriously. We could not have done this without you. Your merciless sword of red-ink rules all! THANK YOU.

To Kay Benjamin: Thank you for believing in a little red-haired girl in your High School English Class. You inspired me to write, and I never stopped. (C.S.)

To Lyric: Thank you for taking our nonsense in stride, and inspiring us to create a new hero for others. With love and always.

And finally...

<u>To our Kickstarter supporters from *The Heart of Hanwi*</u> **<u>project:</u>** Thank you for believing in us and for entrusting us with your names and your memories. We hope we did them justice: Dr. Erin Miracle, Dr. Jon Henner, Denise James, Finley Hislop, Lee Michael Geller.

AFTERWORD

Well, here we are again... at the end of another story.

We hope you all enjoyed this hero's journey and path of discovery in the Realm of Gothika. When we started on this path, Lyric was not our main character. But after several false starts (and some scrapped chapters), we finally decided that we wanted to tell a story about a coming of age in this horror-filled world that we had created. What would that look like? What would they be doing?

And ... like Raise the Dead... awesome cover art coming across Charm's desk inspired our bad guys.

Vampires appear in a multitude of myths and legends across many cultures. We did some deep diving before we decided what myths we wanted to keep and which we wanted to ignore. We knew immediately we did not want *our* vampires to be sexy and appealing. We wanted them to be monsters. More than that, we wanted them to result from human hubris, not a be a curse or a disease.

As with our first Gothika novel (Raise the Dead) – evil is in the eye of the beholder.

And sometimes monsters aren't the worst things out there in the world.

About Us

SandDancer Publications

C.S. Kading and Tony Fuentes have been working together and crafting stories for over two decades. Partners in both mischief and memories, this dynamic duo combines real-world experience with formal education, to bring you stories to tickle your imagination and delight your hearts.

SandDancer was born out of the pandemic and a need to stay sane. We could not enjoy the company of others beyond the safety of our bubble, so we came to you the only other way we could - through books and storytelling.

https://sanddancer.pub/

The Authors

Tony Fuentes

Literary Titan Gold Award-Winning Author

Tony is Renaissance Man in Geek's clothing; not only an author with a weird imagination, but also a painter, gamer, and part-time occultist. With his writing, he tries to spin humor into the world's grounded reality. At the same, he tries to get the audience to look into the stars and dream further beyond. In all things, he strives to give the weird and the wondrous things a place in the world for all to enjoy.

B.S. COMM

Member: IASFA

indie B.R.A.G. Medallion recipient

C.S. Kading

Literary Titan Gold Award-Winning Author

Charmain is a poet, playwright, and storyteller, whose love for writing began in 3rd grade when she won a district writing contest. Her love for fantastical forces motivates her to create stories of heroes, villains, gods, and monsters that often have a foundation in Old World mythology and legends.

MAED

Member: IASFA, IAN

indie B.R.A.G. Medallion recipient

ALSO BY

Check out our works on our website:

SandDancer Publications
https://sanddancer.pub/

The Realm of Gothika

Dark Fantasy
Raise the Dead (a love story)
The Heart of Hanwi

The World of Sanctum Series

Epic Fantasy
Sanctum: Sands of Setesh
Sanctum: Forests of Avalon
Longest Night: A Sanctum Tale

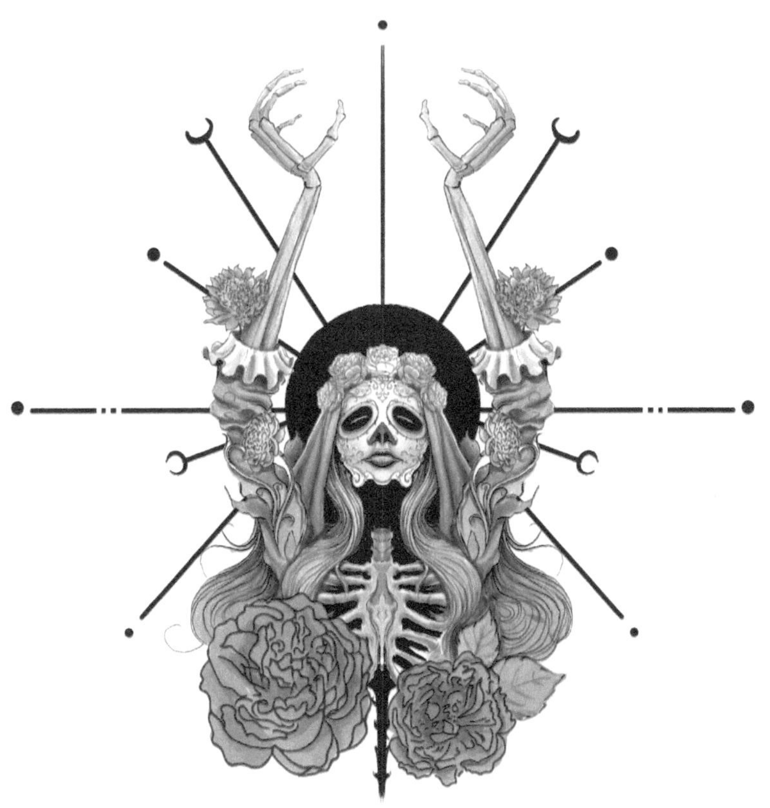